WAR OF THE WORLDS

WAR OF THE WORLDS

How to avoid leading a double life

Adrian Plass

Authentic

17 16 15 14 13 12 11   7 6 5 4 3 2 1

First published 2011 by Authentic Media Limited
52 Presley Way, Crownhill, Milton Keynes, MK8 0ES
www.authenticmedia.co.uk

British Library Cataloguing in Publication Data

A catalogue record for this book is available from the British Library

ISBN: 978-1-85078-956-7

Cover Design by David Smart
Printed and bound by CPI Group (UK) Ltd, Croydon, CR0 4YY

CONTENTS

Introduction

Themes are strange, elusive creatures. One moment they are there in front of you, as clear as clear. All of a sudden, as Bertie Wooster might put it, they seem to flicker, and are gone. As this has been my experience throughout the writing of this book, I thought it would be a good idea to attempt to explain what *War Of The Worlds* is about before you take your first tentative step into Chapter One.

I should begin by saying that almost all the ideas and explorations in this book were born out of reflections arising from the two years my wife and I have spent as community members at Scargill House Conference Centre, just up the road from Kettlewell in North Yorkshire (home of the *Calendar Girls*). Joining a community as 'Writer in Residence' held a particular challenge for me. Travelling and speaking all over the world for twenty-five years has been a very enjoyable, but somewhat isolating experience. How would I get on in the unavoidably exposing ethos of intentional community? It is relatively easy to exude confidence when you stand up in front of groups of people who have come to hear you because they like your books. Was it not possible that cracks and faults would become horribly apparent in this new, intense situation?

Then there was my perception of a loving, laughing, hurting, puzzling, strangely lonely and misunderstood God. Would that hard-won notion survive the religious rough and tumble of community life?

Well, living at Scargill turned out to be challenging in all sorts of ways that I never anticipated, but we would not have missed it for the world. It truly has been a joy for both of us to mix on a daily basis with community members and with guests, and to find a valid role in both of these contexts. It is undoubtedly true that there have been times when all we wanted was to run or drive screaming out of the gates, and I think I love my own space far too much to live in this way for the rest of my life. But yes, I am reassured and warmed by the way in which the core of myself has somehow remained intact in day-to-day interaction with a bunch of (mainly) lovely people who simply cannot avoid one another.

And God? Ah, that, or rather he, is the reason for this book. Close, ongoing ministry with all sorts of folk over the last two years has made me more certain than ever that authenticity in individuals and churches is essential if we honestly do want to see the Holy Spirit working supernaturally in men and women, and loving them to life. To make this possible we may have to go to war. What kind of war, and for what reason?

The war in individuals is a conflict between the world of inside and the world of outside. Jesus does not call people to deny what they feel and think and fear and yearn for. He calls them to tell the truth and to discover a freedom that is the more spectacularly satisfying because it deals with all that we are, instead of an edited version of ourselves. It is a battle between giving in to the shame of inadequacy, and understanding that the one imperfect sacrifice that God will gladly receive from us is our flawed selves. We are called, not to be wonderful Christians, but obedient failures. We may be asked to co-operate with God as he works on changing aspects of our personalities, but in the meantime there is work to be done and, if we wish, he will use us to do it.

The planets warring with each other in the church are interesting, because there are times when they look oddly similar. In both worlds, you will see what appears to be spiritual fire. In one world, the fire is from God and has real power: in the other, it is fabricated by man and is impotent and misleading. On one planet there are words and music and patterns and claims, that appear to demonstrate a real concern for the desires of the heart of God, but are actually hollow and virtually meaningless. On the other, these things are filled with the sincere aspirations of those who know that they are weak and can do nothing, but who also believe that God is strong and can do anything. In one world suffering, damaged people are told that they can find release and healing if they become committed citizens, but are actually not allowed freedom to properly express their pain and are forced to role-play healing. In the other, the care never shuts people down. It opens them up and stays with them exactly as they are for as long as is needed. On one planet, dangerously open spaces are filled quickly before God has a chance to get in: on the other, there are large areas left for God to stretch his muscles as much and in any way that he wants.

Enough. My theme is beginning to do that flickering thing. Lots of laughs and tears in this book. I do hope you enjoy it. What shall we start with? I know, just to cheer ourselves up, let's consider the subject of Death.

One

Death

As I have pointed out on many occasions, if you scratch a Christian you will generally find a human being. But why is there a need to scratch? What are we afraid of, and which fears are allayed or hidden by these carapaces of carefully controlled religious observance or mindless, unconsidered optimism? Is it the case that we as a church push away the dread of inevitable darkness just as the rest of the world does, but through the employment of different means? We would-be followers of Jesus are going to have to accept that we are solidly in the life and death business, especially if we wish to respond to the call of Jesus in the fourth chapter of John's Gospel when he calls us to become labourers and give him a hand with the harvest.

Almost nobody wishes to embrace death, but in the granular world of spiritual reality we must.

Heading for the grave?

Let's start with me moaning about getting closer to actually experiencing it.

Writers of Christian satire know that this genre is likely to involve an element of risk, particularly if they recognise the need to retain a cutting edge. Some you win, some you lose, that's what experience suggests, but when you think about it, that's what risk is all about. And this death business is a good example.

As I approach my sixty-third birthday, I find that death is working its grinning way fairly quickly up the queue of concerns that continually dogs my glorious, faith-filled life. Getting older is a pain. I don't want to. I don't like it. Now that I've finally begun to do a bit of sensible prioritising of activities in my life, it seems ridiculous that I'm not going to have much longer to put them into practice. Here is a silly poem that expresses some of my current angst.

You know you're getting old

You know you're getting old when an attractive woman crinkles her eyes playfully, calls you 'Young Man', and asks with a little rippling laugh if you'd like to be her toy-boy

When most of the parties you go to are gatherings of cadaverous or plump people sitting like grey statues in the same chairs all evening drinking two thirds of a gloomy glass of wine, and talking about the value of their houses and the state of their legs

When no-one asks for proof that you qualify for Senior Citizen rates at National Trust properties

When men in their mid-thirties with black-rimmed spectacles and resonant voices who steeple their hands tell you that you still have a lot to offer

When you find yourself deeply fascinated by the fact that 'love' is an anagram of 'vole'

When the nearest you get to a night on the tiles is a game of Scrabble

When you know precisely which part of your mouth you're eating with

When a trip upstairs is a journey into the unknown

When, having arrived upstairs, you find yourself in a bathroom, and realise that it could be any bathroom, anywhere in the world

When everyone else in the universe believes that most of your problems can be solved with a cup of tea, and all the rest with a digestive biscuit

When you feel threatened by young people with long upper bodies and peaked caps turned backwards who hit tennis balls ferociously

When you start drooling and cooing and aaahing over a baby buggy before checking that there's a baby in it

When your children try to persuade you to spend money on yourself instead of on them

The impenetrable wall

Mildly humorous as those grim indicators of doom might be, the eventual death of someone we love is, generally speaking, a horrible thing. Bereavement can seem a hopelessly high, solid and impenetrable wall. There's nothing you can do about it, no way in which you can climb it or indeed change any aspect of it. And it is frequently made worse by crass comments or behaviour from those of us who simply cannot or will not conquer our own feelings of fear and inadequacy when we are faced with the harrowing pain of bereavement in others. All of the unhelpful comments in the piece that follows were kindly contributed by folk who endured them at one time or another. There are other, worse ones that I have not included. Some you would not believe. Many tell me stories of friends, acquaintances and fellow church members actually crossing the road to avoid the awkwardness of an encounter with such raw sorrow. Let's be honest about this. Most of us have been guilty of such neglect at some point in our lives, often because we simply do not know what to say or how to behave.

And that is why (in my view) it has been worth the risk of reading and presenting 'Have You Moved On Yet?' in public. For the vast majority of those who have suffered loss, it has had a liberating effect, not despite but because of the moments of humour arising from the text. One or two have found it upsetting. The point, though, is that it offers an opportunity to talk about helpful ways of relating to folk who are wrestling with the agony of loss. Here are just a few suggestions that have been made.

I really want to talk about the person I've lost. Please ask me.
Just be there. You don't have to do anything special.
Don't try to solve my problem or dilute my pain with hollow religion or false optimism. It won't work.
Don't be afraid to laugh with me. I need to keep those muscles working.
Meet my eyes, otherwise I shall end up comforting you.

Try not to be afraid of me. I need you.
Make me an apple pie.

Our friend Liz has been very helpful in thinking about these things. Liz was devastated by the death of her husband Ian. He was original, creative, enormously kind-hearted and extremely knowledgeable. Bridget and I met with Liz at her home on the first anniversary of Ian's death. Among other things we talked about the interesting variety of clichés that bereaved people have to put up with. From Liz's point of view, the worst was the one that I've used as the title for this piece.

Have you moved on yet?

Have you moved on yet?
No, I have not moved on. I have not moved at all. I've been like the two disciples on the road to Emmaus, standing still and looking sad. If by any chance I have moved infinitesimally, it is most likely that I have moved off, as opposed to on

She's just slipped into the next room
The next room? Slipped into the next room? She's been in the next room for the last eight years. I've nursed her and fed her and read to her and watched her dying in the next room. I can assure you that she is not in the next room any more. She's not in any room. I've looked. I've searched. She's somewhere else

Time is a great healer
Not for him, it wasn't

Do you know, my uncle died of exactly the same thing
That is a huge comfort

Well, he had a good innings
You don't know much about cricket, do you? When you have a good innings you don't want it to end. In fact, the nearer you get to the magic of a century, the more determined you are to get that last sweet boundary. One hundred runs – or more! Now, that's a good innings

She's gone before
No, definitely the first time, never went before, never dead before, always alive before

At least he's in heaven now, so he's happy and at peace
Gosh! I do so admire theological certainty. Do you have as much faith for yourself as you have for him?

She's in a much better place
Thank you. This was quite a nice place when she was here. Actually, it was a very nice place. I'm afraid I never did realise just how nice it was

I know exactly how you feel
Do you?

In a way it's for the best
For the best? Whose best? My best? Your best? The Duke of Edinburgh's best? Shirley Bassey's best? It's not for the best. It's for the worst

He didn't suffer at the end
No, and I'm glad. But I did. I suffered

She wouldn't want you to grieve
Okay, I won't then. Actually, I think she might be a bit disappointed if I remained – totally unmoved. What do you think?

You mustn't blame yourself
Mustn't I? Well, I do. I do blame myself. I blame myself for all sorts of things. I blame myself for not telling her I loved her three million more times than I did. For not changing the little things in me that would have made all the difference. I blame myself for things I did and didn't do. Commission, omission, all sorts of things. Yes, whether I must or mustn't blame myself – I do

He's with you now just as much as he ever was
No, he's not

You'll be able to join her soon
Ah, right, I'd better cancel tomorrow's milk then

Gethsemane, suffering and prayer for release

The effects of death and disaster are felt by many people, including Christians, in all sorts of ways. How should believers pray about suffering? The things we know about what happened to Jesus in the garden of Gethsemane might offer some unwanted guidance. One set of words that he uttered there have been rolling round and round my mind over the last few months.

'The sorrow in my heart is so great that it almost crushes me.'

Terrible, lonely words, are they not? The Saviour of the world, this man who, mysteriously, was also God, came close to being crushed by fear and sorrow while his friends dozed a few yards away. In other words, he was on the edge of failure. No wonder he made a last plea to be released from the horror that was to come. 'Father, if it is your will, let this cup be removed from me.'

Clearly it was perfectly legitimate for Jesus to ask for the cup of suffering to be taken from him, but only if he was fully prepared to accept the possibility that it couldn't be. And indeed it couldn't. As an act of obedience he was required to face intense pain, humiliation, and separation from his Father at the moment when he needed him most. The lesson is stark and uncompromising and clear. We can ask God to remove any cup of suffering that doesn't appeal to us. There is nothing wrong with that. But if that cup of sorrow is essential to his plans for us, others or the world, we will be asked to drain it, even if it is a matter of gritting our teeth and acting purely out of obedience. It will be hard. Of course it will. As Jesus himself will reiterate to us one day over a convivial cup of ambrosia (not rice), the spirit may be willing, but the flesh is weak.

Have you ever come close to being crushed by sorrow? I expect you have. God has. We are all in this together, so let's try to stay awake for each other.

In good company

For the disciples of Jesus, the Saturday following his horrible death must have been a thick mist of disappointment and darkness. I have been through the pain of losing people I love very much, but my response to the death of my grandmother when I was six years old may have been the nearest I have come to understanding what the disciples went through.

How could such a bright light be put out? What on earth did it mean, this death thing? Why had such an important part of my life been snatched away from me for no good reason that I could see? How would the heavy black shadow that settled in my stomach at the moment when I heard the news ever be dispersed? Sometimes, as the weeks went by, it was not a shadow. It was a vicious mystery with sharp edges that had cut mercilessly into normality. There are still occasions, more than fifty years later, when that wound opens. A hatred and a dread of death are part of what I am, and will probably remain so for the rest of my life. However, there are no worlds at war over this issue as far as I'm concerned. I need no ministry for my condition, thank you very much. As we have seen, there is little doubt that Jesus hated death as well, so I'm in good company.

Here is one of those bereaved, soul-sick disciples lost in the fog of that terrible weekend.

The disciple who was dreading Sunday

I do not understand.

Lord Jesus, if my words rise before you on this dark and pain-filled Saturday evening, please hear my heart crying out to you that I do not understand. I do not believe that a single one of us understands. We, your disciples, wait behind these locked doors like dead things, like dumb pieces of lumber that have been leant carelessly against the wall or discarded upon the floor because they no longer have a function. Our minds burn with a thousand questions, and they are all the same question. Why has the flower failed to bloom? Why has the wine turned to water? Why have our wounds reopened? Why has hope turned to despair? Where is light and leadership? Where are you? Master, where *are* you? You are not here with us.

You forbade swords at Gethsemane, Lord Jesus. Swords away, you commanded. No defence. If you wished, you could call on your father and he would put more than twelve legions of angels at your disposal. That's what you said. Twelve legions? Well, then, why not? Why not? How are we simple people to understand that in your strange, upside down view of heaven and earth, it is more fruitful to fail and die and abandon your friends, than to succeed and live and triumph over the very present forces of evil? I recall some words you once spoke:

'Unless a kernel of wheat falls to the ground and dies, it remains only a single seed. But if it dies it produces many seeds.'

A good picture. A truth to be stored and considered. Kernels of wheat do indeed produce many seeds. But, Lord, you were not a kernel of wheat. You were a man. Now you are dead. And one dead man does not produce a harvest of living men. Does he?

You are in a tomb, and we, your living servants, are entombed in grief. We long to see your face. We yearn for your voice. Lacking your wisdom and power, how can we continue? The future is a desert. As night draws in we

shall try to sleep, but the mockery of morning will surely
come. Lord Jesus, my eyes fill with tears. How am I to face
tomorrow without you?

Dank and dreadful

You will not be surprised to hear that, as well as hating
death, I have always hated going to funerals or memorial
services, especially the ones that are held in those dreadful teak-infested, barn-like erections where the atmosphere is soaked with dark brown gloom, and you know
that it all has to be over in twenty minutes because a dole-
ful queue of penguin-like mourning groups is building
up in the heartlessly ornate gardens outside. I never
know what to think or feel or do. It's all so dank and
dreadful. Worst, perhaps, is the certain knowledge that
most of the people I have loved and lost would blink
incredulously or even laugh heartily at the incongruity
between the way they actually were and the way in which
their loss is marked. Don't get me wrong. I have never felt
any inclination to leap about on the edges of the graves of
those I love singing songs of joy and celebration. As I
have already said, death scares me. I am sickened by it,
just as Jesus was, and the promise of heaven is a rickety
raft that only just keeps me afloat on such storm-tossed
occasions.

The fact is that, being so severely afflicted with the twin
diseases of whimsy and flippancy, I do have a tendency to
drift off into all manner of bizarre fantasies in the middle
of the most solemn ceremonies. The other day, for
instance, I found myself standing among a group of forty
or fifty mourners as the coffin-encased body of an old

friend was lowered slowly into its gruesome earthen cavity. Such a tidy and perfectly shaped receptacle, I reflected, for the inchoate reality of death. Gripped by a spasm of emotional disgust, I turned my eyes away and sought distraction in a subtle scan of the crowd that surrounded me. As I did so a question formed in my mind. What if one of those horribly energetic, rather impatient wedding photographers with the spring-loaded legs had been hired to record this event? How might he have organised and addressed this black clad throng?

The funeral photographer

'Okay, close family of the dead please – no, I said *close* family, didn't I? You three back off. Yes, and you. Off you go. No, not you! You! You come in! Look, can we get on? I've got another three funerals today. Can you just – thank you! Right! Nnnnice! (*CLICK! CLICK! CLICK!*) Now, friends of the dead please. If you're family you can't be friends, can you? No, I haven't got time to argue. Friends of the dead – over here. No, you lot clear off now. Yes, go on! Friends of the dead lined up behind the grave please. Come on, quick march, fall in! Not literally. Ha-ha! Small ones at the front. Tall ones at the back. Close in at the ends. Let's get co-o-o-osy! Right. (*CLICK!*) Sorry folks, but can we just get the smiles off our faces, it's supposed to be a funeral after all. Still one or two smiling. Come on! Think of the dear deceased, cold and dead in that box. Think tears, think grief, think sad, sad, sad! That's better. That is beautiful! (*CLICK! CLICK! CLICK!*) Thank *you!* Now, nice big group picture. In you all come. Vicar in the centre. Lots of compassion tinged with hope please, Reverend.

You know the drill. No, I want you to look compassionate, not as if you're about to throw up. Church at its best and all that. Nice strong mix of dignity and empathy. Yes, *good!* Oh, *very* nice! *(CLICK! CLICK! CLICK!)* Right, that just about winds it up. Someone just remind me of the name so I don't end up sending your pics to last Tuesday's christening party. Ha-ha!'

Letter to Rob Frost

Funerals are dark and uncomfortable, but they are only part of the overall disconnect that happens when we are trying to face the total disappearance of those we have loved. Perhaps this is particularly true when the individual concerned was an exceptionally vivid personality. You can't see them, but you can't *not* see them either, if you know what I mean. You probably don't. I don't think I do, but I know it means something important.

Talking of vivid personalities, a few years ago I was asked if I would like to say something at Rob Frost's memorial service. I had known Rob for some years, mainly as the inspirational leader of Easter People, the Methodist festival enjoyed by thousands of people in a variety of venues across the United Kingdom. I was very fond of Rob. Unfortunately, because of a previous engagement, it was not possible for me to get to the service in person, but I was able to send a contribution for someone else to read. What form was it to take? After a lot of worrying and wondering I decided to write him a letter. I don't know who read it out in the end. I wasn't there. But Rob was. He heard it.

Dear Rob,

You're in heaven now, so I can be as rude as I like. Before I ever met you I saw a photograph of your face in a magazine. It wasn't a very good likeness and I can remember thinking that you looked like a demented squirrel. Later I came to realise that this wasn't so far off the mark. You and Jesus and the average demented squirrel always did have one main feature in common, the expenditure of enormous energy and passion in the quest to save as many nuts as possible. You were a Jesus nut, weren't you Rob? Whether you were elated or in despair, exhausted or refreshed, encouraged or disappointed, you never lost the desire to see people waking up to the fact that Jesus is whatever light is needed in every conceivable kind of darkness.

My memories of you are like snapshots.

I remember being on stage when you were speaking. You'd asked me to have a few bits and pieces ready so that you could have little breaks when you ran out of steam. After the second of these preaching stretches you turned away from the microphone and walked towards me at the back of the stage, your face pallid and strained from the sheer passion of communication, your eyes almost crossed with exhaustion.

'Go and do something,' you gasped, 'I'm all preached out . . .'

I remember travelling to do a performance for Lantern Arts, and learning when I arrived that my wife, Bridget, had been involved in a serious accident on the motorway on her way to join me. The love and practical concern that you and Jacquie offered on that nerve-jangling evening is something that I shall never forget.

And I remember sitting on the stage at Easter People in a little semi-circle of people who were going to contribute during the week. You asked us to explain, one by one, why we had come. One person said that he was there because he wanted to see Jesus lifted up and worshipped. Another talked about how he hoped to see the Kingdom increased. The third expressed an aim to see Almighty God glorified. And so it went on. It was all very impressive. I was last. I was at a bit of a loss. There wasn't much left for me to say really. All the good stuff had been pinched.

'And why are you here, Adrian?' you asked.

'For the money,' I replied.

You pretended to be shocked.

'I sincerely hope not!' you exclaimed, 'I'll have to see Marian afterwards. We must be paying you too much.'

But you weren't paying us too much, Rob. You weren't paying us too little either, but that wasn't the point. None of us ever did things for you because of the money. We did them because you had one of the greatest gifts of all, the ability to show people that you truly valued them. Lots of snapshots there. Mini-memories of faces lighting up as you greeted each and every individual as though they were the most important person in the world. And you know something, Rob, that was what made things like Easter People so very special. Because that attitude trickled down and affected every aspect of the festival. There were never any second-class Christians at Easter People. What an achievement.

So now you've gone pioneering off to find out if all the stuff we talk about is true. You and I were always going to spend more time together, weren't we, Rob? An evening or two in one of those cosy Sussex pubs that I was always telling you about. It'll have to wait now, but on the new earth the beer will be even better, surely. I'd better let you go now. You're probably in the middle of persuading Gabriel to take charge of car-parking at some massive divine event. Thanks for all you were and are, Rob. I'll miss you. See you later. Cheers, mate. Love, Adrian.

What kind of resurrection?

The physical death of Rob Frost or anyone else that we have loved can be unspeakably painful. What a day it will be when we meet again. However, there is more than one kind of death, and there are times when we have to choose whether we want to be resurrected or not, and in what sense.

I have known people who are confronted by the sudden realisation that a view or position they have been gripping with both hands is about to be snatched away by experience or circumstances. It can be a spirit-crunching shock. How are we to deal with the prospect of losing a part of ourselves that has been a crucial aspect of the way in which we present an identity to our outer and inner worlds? This is a critical question, for instance, for those who routinely deny the authenticity of faith and then encounter God in such an undeniable way that a radical decision has to be made. I suppose there are two options, and both involve a form of resurrection.

The first is a kind of false resurrection. It is possible to step back or away from the loss and the pain and the risk and the possibilities of the new. You can just about do it. Bury truth in the deepest grave that your heart offers and perform some urgent artificial respiration on the mistake that sustained you.

Saul of Tarsus had a go at doing this, didn't he? Do you remember his testimony to Agrippa in Acts 26? He describes how the power of God knocked him off his horse, and Jesus said the following memorable words: 'Saul, Saul, why do you persecute me? It is hard for you to kick against the goads.' Saul had been denying his own heart for some time, but was well and truly ambushed by God on that life-changing, world-altering day.

The second option is to go for the bona fide resurrection, to embrace the change, go for the risk, head for the light. There is a kind of death involved, and possibly a hefty price to pay, but there is also a second birth and the promise of spiritual authenticity. Is it worth it? I'll let you know. Birth hurts.

Most of us don't have such dramatically unavoidable Damascus Road experiences as Saul. Many are still in denial. Here's a man who has to make that choice I have just been talking about. Old or new? False or true? What kind of resurrection is it to be?

The man who served wine at the Last Supper

I was at that Last Supper.

I don't get mixed up with stuff at work. Never have. It's not my way. It's hard enough living in one world, let alone two or three, like some idiots. Home is my world. There are enough problems there without getting tangled up with my pompous master or his greedy guests or any of those peasants who earn a crust in the same house as me. Mind you, I'm not saying I don't do my job properly. I do.

I work hard for my wages. Move furniture, wait at tables, clear things away, anything I'm asked to do within reason. Just don't ask me to get involved. Blank face, cold heart. That's me.

I might leave. Last night was weird, and I don't do weird.

Here's the picture, right. Yet another religious nutcase impresses my gullible master enough to get the use of his best room for a night. There he sits like a little king surrounded by as motley a crew of dippy disciples as you've ever seen in your life, and my job is to keep the wine flowing. No problem. Done it a hundred times.

All right. I'll tell you. Only ever going to say it once, but I'll tell you. Rabbi holds the cup out after the meal. I start to fill it. Wine pours like wine has always poured. Everything goes dark in my head. Blackness turns to rich red. Whole building shudders. World tearing itself apart. Creaking, grinding, roaring, groaning. Millions of tons of rock splitting, cracking, shattering. Me spinning through chaos looking for somewhere to land. Explosion of light. Peace. Back to normal. The rabbi's cup is filled.

End of. Weird. I might leave.

Two

Prayer

There are probably no right or wrong ways of praying. When it comes from the heart it sings. However, it is a sad fact that many Christians find prayer more difficult as they get older. What kinds of battle will need to be fought if we are to capture ground for honest communication with God? A request from my daughter set me thinking.

The language of prayer

As I write, Kate is two-thirds through her first year as a teacher of dance and choreography at a Catholic secondary school in Newcastle upon Tyne. Soon after her year began, she asked if I could help her to put together something for a school assembly. The theme was the problem of being led astray by peer pressure, and the presentation needed to include a prayer that could be said by one of her students and understood by the others. Having composed the prayer that appears below, I realised that in aiming for words and structures and ideas that might appeal more to young people, I had actually written something that could be easily and honestly used by just about anybody.

Why does it take me so long to learn these lessons? Years ago, when I was working with children of mixed ages in a Residential Care situation, I got all the kids together to talk about a small transistor radio (remember them?) that had been taken from the staff office. I felt absolutely sure that this 'major' crime had been committed by one of the smallest children, an eight-year-old boy called Richard. Accordingly, when I addressed the group, I made sure that my tone and language were carefully adjusted to that age-group.

'Right,' I said, avoiding actually looking at Richard and sounding like a slightly sterner, but warmly avuncular version of Joyce Grenfell (remember her?), 'let me tell you why I've called you all together. I'm sorry to say that somebody – *somebody* has taken the little black radio out of the office, and I think that person knows who I'm talking about.' I paused impressively. 'So, here's what I would like that person to do. When this meeting is finished I want you to go off and get that radio from the place where you've hidden it, and then bring it to me and say sorry, and we'll say no more about it. But if you *don't* do that – well, *I'll* be coming to see *you*, and I can tell you that I shall be very, very cross. *Very* cross! And you won't enjoy that, will you?'

They filed away in silence and ten minutes later there was a gentle knock on the office door. In stumbled a tough eighteen-year-old boy called Russ with a sheepish expression on his face, and a small black radio clutched in his hand. My talk had worked. Right tone, right language, wrong suspect. If I had thought the culprit was Russ I would not have tackled him via a public meeting, and I would definitely not have used such a simple approach.

Perhaps there is something similar to be learned about our attempts to pray. I enjoy many liturgical prayers simply because I love beautifully written prose with a heart in it, but surely the time has come to free ourselves from the awkward, pseudo religious inanities that we find ourselves bleating out in so-called open prayer sessions. God must find it very disappointing that quite animated discussions between Christians tend to be closely followed by a prayer session in which normal, heartfelt communication is replaced by dull mantras and unsmiling petitions, delivered in artificial, slightly weird language forms.

Change in this area does take a lot of practice, of course. Apart from anything else, for some folk there is the largely unspoken issue of whether they believe that the God they are speaking to actually exists. A trivial but possibly important point. Speaking out loud to someone you can't see is profoundly self-revealing in this respect.

Anyway, we shall push on with our attempts to be as warm and chatty with God as we are with our friends, and see what happens. In Matthew 6, Jesus suggests retiring to our rooms so that we can speak to our Father in private. Good idea, and a very good place to practice being normal.

This is the prayer that I wrote for Kate's girls to use in her assembly.

A prayer about being strong and not being led astray

Father God, most of the time we do sort of want to be good, and we want to make the right decisions about the things we do and the way we behave. Sometimes, though, it's really, really difficult. What we're frightened of is that we might end up feeling silly, standing on the edge of the rest of the crowd because we said no to joining in with stuff that we know would be bad for us. We don't like being laughed at, in fact we hate it, and it's so hard when you feel you're being left out. Could you help us please? Could you help us to be stronger and more brave when we have to make these difficult choices? Inside we know that they could change what happens to us for the rest of our lives. Thank you for listening to us and standing beside us and telling us it's all right to be who we are, instead of being soft and giving in and turning into what other people seem to think we ought to be. Thank you very much, Father God. Amen.

Not a happy bunny?

Speaking of retreating into our rooms to speak to God, it is my strong belief that we are able to say anything that is on our minds in this private, familial situation. I say this because I know from dismal experience that there are times when we simply cannot trust that God could possibly be willing to hear from crap-buckets like us.

One of the most necessary and most difficult things for us human beings to believe is that, with God, there are a million new beginnings available for stricken losers like me and countless other refugees from the gloomy lands of darkness and difficulty. I suppose one of the problems is that when we are wading knee-deep through some species of experiential excrement, it is almost impossible to give head-room to the notion that this very same excrement might be regarded very differently by keen gardeners, who would probably call it manure. I am no gardener, but I gather that you can grow things in manure. Roses, for instance. My favourite flower.

The ways of God are mysterious, not to say extremely odd, but the history of his dealings with suffering, sinful people makes interesting reading. Sometimes he heals minds or bodies or spirits – or all three. Sometimes he doesn't. Why is that? Ah, what an incredible bestseller I could write if the Lord would give me one incontrovertible answer to that question. I do have an idea or two, and you might well have several, but I have only one thing to say in this connection. Deep in my heart or spirit, or wherever it is that one is most sure of things, I am convinced that this compassionate, playful, persevering, ingenious, suffering, kindly God does not want *anyone* to be trapped in prisons of the past, and is always looking for ways to make freedom possible. So it might be worth having a go. It might be worth talking to him openly and honestly about what has happened and what you need. Yes, of course he knows anyway, but we all like to be talked to by people we love. If you're more or less okay, why not petition on behalf of someone else? You might be amazed.

What do you want most in the world? Tell God. Is it really difficult for you to forgive yourself? Join the club, and tell God. Is it your experience that God fails to turn up sometimes? Tell him how much that upsets you, and ask him what it means. He won't mind. If you feel unsure about talking to God like this, then read the psalms, starting with Psalm 88. That'll make you feel better. Whoever wrote that jolly little poem was not a happy bunny . . .

One more comment on this subject, and on the general subject of worlds warring against each other in the context of Christian living. Not too long ago Bridget and I met a young woman who was in her late teens. She had the look of someone who is postponing the rest of her life until some great problem is solved. This turned out to be precisely the case. Rachel's father had died when she was eight years old. That event and the feelings it produced in her had never been properly processed, as far as she was concerned. She came from a church family which was clearly caring, but equally clearly was unable to resist the temptation to set about 'fixing' the negative outcome of Rachel's bereavement.

The world inside Rachel was dark and angry and disappointed, and, perhaps above all, deeply bewildered. What was going on? This God she had been told about, the one who was supposed to love and care for her and was interested in every tiny detail of her life, had taken her father away from her when she was little. Why? Why had he let her down so badly when she needed him most? It wasn't right and it wasn't fair and she would like the chance to tell him exactly what she thought of his bungling, thoughtless act of neglect. She wanted her father here, now, so that she could talk to him and ask his advice and lean on him at difficult times.

The world presented by those well-meaning people who had advised Rachel over the years was rather different.

God always has a purpose, and, although we cannot understand it now, that will have been the case with the death of Rachel's father.

Good, love-enhancing things can arise out of such tragedies. Wait and see.

God suffered as much as she did. Knowing that will help the grieving process.

Jesus is our rock, and she should rest on and in him.

The tantalising thing is that I agree with every one of these notions, and I would certainly say them to anyone who is ready to hear them. That is the point, though. When these bad things happen, there has got to be a time when the suffering victim is allowed to feel what they feel, think what they think, say whatever they want to say to God. That's how I had felt when my grandmother died. It doesn't matter a monkey's elbow if the inchoate cry we let out is theologically unsound, or disrespectful or illogical or just a tear-stained mess. That is the world in which we find ourselves, and that is the world where we need to be met. God can handle it. In fact, like all good fathers, he would rather see it all come out for the sake of the person he loves. Meeting people where they are is a bit of a speciality of his, as Jesus can testify. This desire to 'fix' people is a bit of a disease in the modern church. We can't do it. Only God can. Isn't it difficult, though?

Holding the balance

Holding this balance between naked honesty and faith in God can appear to be a tricky business, but, as Jesus so helpfully said, 'The truth will set you free.' A lot of Christian music is impenetrably optimistic, which is odd when you consider the contrasts of mood found in the Bible, but surely it must be possible to combine vulnerability with hope and tentative faith. I've had a go with the following lyrics. They are an expansion of one of the finest petitions in the old prayer book. What do you think?

Lighten our darkness

Lighten our darkness, we beseech thee, oh, Lord,
In the name of your Son, Jesus Christ,
For we know there will be troubles,
Before we see the morning light,
So, defend us, Lord defend us, oh, defend us,
From the dangers of the night.

For dangers there will be,
There never was a mystery,
He said so,
The passion of the Son,
Has only just begun,
He said so,
If courage is what we lack,
We'd better be turning back,
We know that, Lord, but tonight,
We're feeling lonely.

Lighten our darkness . . .

As long as we can stand,
Like children hand in hand,
Together,
We'll see the tale unfold,
And love will make us bold,
Together,
Together we stand today,
Tomorrow is far away,
But sometimes we long to know,
The end of the story.

Lighten our darkness . . .

Staying in touch

It can take a lifetime to wake up to the fact that however much we have sinned, and however many mistakes we have made, God would much rather hear from us than be avoided like the plague. It used to be like that with banking.

My wife and I have been with the same high street bank for more than forty years, and, my goodness, how things have changed. Until a couple of decades ago, the local bank manager was far more autonomous, and much more likely to become something approximating to a family friend. When my wife Bridget and I were in our poverty-stricken twenties and early thirties (as opposed to our poverty-stricken early sixties) we had a number of nervous encounters with pleasantly avuncular managers who were able to be stern or encouraging as the occasion (or our gruesomely mismanaged finances) demanded. Bridget tended to cry, which was always useful, while I, suitably rueful and repentant, did a nice line in nodding slowly and seriously.

These helpful gentlemen invariably made the same point. Something can always be arranged *as long as you stay in touch.* Problems with our spindly bank account were amplified and actually made more problematic when we hid from the issue, and even (oh, the guilt of it) walked through the town a different way so that we didn't have to pass the bank. Those slightly uncomfortable interviews in the manager's office always produced a result, a plan, a way forward, at the very least some respite from the pressure of imminent disaster.

As I have said, experience suggests that the same thing applies to our encounters with God. *As long as we stay in touch* something can be arranged. If I know that I am on the cusp of succumbing to temptation, there is almost certainly a little war raging in me. If I take my dilemma to God or one of his representatives, I might lose the opportunity to plunge pleasantly into whatever is beckoning me so seductively. On the other hand, there is a part of me that really does want to be an obedient child of God. Which shall I do? Well, as a friend said to me once, most of life is a choice between what we don't want and what we *really* don't want. For better or worse, when I look honestly into my soul I shall know which is which.

So ask yourself this. What would make you want to visit the divine bank manager? Is it because he loves you, or because you love him? And where is he? Maybe we're getting too carried away here. After all, if God's love is eternal and unchangeable, does it really matter if you don't take his views and plans on board? He'll still feel the same about you, won't he?

If you want to be depressed and challenged all at the same time, have a look in 2 Samuel 11–18, the story of King David (a man after God's own heart!), who committed adultery with Bathsheba, and then made heartless arrangements for the murder of Uriah, her husband. When could he have stopped the rot? What happened because he didn't? Why did he not stay in touch, and what were the consequences?

Prayer in action

Here's a fellow who, like most of us, has a lot to learn about prayer. Somehow, he has contacted God on the telephone.

GOD : Hello, God here, did you call?
BILL : Wow! Is that really God? I mean – you know, God-God?
G : Yes, it's God. It really is – God-God.
B : Sorry, thing is, we used to sing a song in church with the children about prayer being like a telephone, but I never heard of anyone actually –

G : No, well, it isn't usually, but this time it is. So, what can I do for you?

B : This is weird! I always thought you'd sound like – you know – Morgan Freeman.

G : Sorry to disappoint you. We couldn't afford him. Who *do* I sound like?

B : Er, actually, you sound a bit like my wife.

G : Yes, well, that figures. Probably the nearest you're likely to get to hearing directly from me. So – what can I do for you?

B : Ah, right, yes. Right. Heh, just a minute, I suppose, technically, I'm praying now, aren't I?

G : Well, you're talking to me, if that's what you mean.

B : Ah, right. Okay. Right! Right. Lord, I just want to just ask you if, in your great mercy you could just help me to just find a way to just –

G : Excuse me, excuse me. Sorry. Why have you closed your eyes? Why are you speaking in that silly, soupy voice? And why are you just-just-just-just-justing like a defective lawnmower?

B : What? Er, well, I closed my eyes because we usually do when we pray. And I spoke in that particular voice because we tend to speak in that particular voice when we pray, and I just-just-just-just-justed because er, I dunno. I just happen to just do that when I just – pray.

G : *Just* – talk to me.

B : Right. Okay. Right. Right. Well, it's about my son, Paul.

G : Oh, yes, I know Paul. Nice lad.

B : Oh! You think so? Well, you don't have to live with – anyway, what I wanted to ask was this. I'd like him and me to have a better, deeper relationship, and I just – I mean – I thought that if I were to just – if I were to pray

for him for a solid hour every day, *you* might, you know
. . .
G : Look, take him down to the recreation ground and –
B : I mean, I know I've not been the best of pray-ers over
the years, but if you could just let the Holy Spirit enter into
the – the . . .
G : Get him a new bat and some stumps and spend some
time –
B : You know, enter into the heart of my prayer, and
redemptively transfigure our relationship, I promise that-
that-that praise for your name will be ever on my lips.
G : No, it won't. In any case, what you need to do is get
down the rec and show him that –
B : Hear me, Lord, as I cry to thee, and grant that peace
which giveth us rest in thy bosom!
G : Oh, please! Not pseudo-sixteenth century English. And
you can leave my bosom out of it. Listen, I *have* heard your
words and I've clearly suggested you spend an hour playing cricket with Paul instead of spending the same amount
of time talking to me in a funny voice and making promises you can't keep. I can't play cricket with him. You can.
What you don't seem to realise is that I'm as keen on –
B : (*sings wildly*) I'm H-A-P-P-Y, I'm H-A-P-P-Y, I think I am,
I know I am, I'm H-A-P-P-Y! I'm –
G : (*as he begins to sing*) Oh, no, not that one! Please not
that one! Anything but that one!
(*closes phone and exits*)
B : (*realising there's no-one there*) Oh! Oh, well.
WIFE : (*entering*) What are you doing?
B : I've been talking to God on the tele – I mean, I've been
praying about Paul and me getting on better and –
W : I told you. Take him out on the field for a game of

something. That's what he needs. Don't turn it into a big spiritual thing. I'm always saying that.

B : (*thoughtfully*) You don't sound anything like Morgan Freeman, you know.

Something silly

Let's finish this section with something even sillier, shall we? It might even be silly enough to really mean something. My wife and I were in the car the other day when an Anglican Church service began on the radio. It involved a set of prayers read by a bishop who was obviously suffering from the pandemic Anglican disease of alliteration. It made us laugh and we decided to make up one of our own. This is it.

Alliterative prayer

We remember those who are depressed, deserted, disappointed, disenchanted or despairing. We pray indeed for all who suffer from things beginning with 'D'. Dante-fetishism, drooling, defeat at dominoes, disembowelment, dysfunctional dongles, dyspepsia, dyslexia, distemper, disco-fever, Derren Browne, disestablishmentarianism, discombobulation, dissolution, destitution, diminution and Ken Dodd . . .

Grace at conferences

Inspired by the creation of this wonderful piece of literature, I decided to have a go at writing my own version of those lengthy prayers said before meals at Christian conference centres, the ones that try to thank God for absolutely *everyone* involved with preparation of the meal. It does go on a bit, but – hey, what's new?

Lord, we thank you for those who have served this food, those who have prepared and cooked it, we remember those who delivered it to this place, and those who packed and loaded it in readiness for that delivery. We thank you for the ones who transported the raw ingredients to the place from which it was delivered, and those who loaded those ingredients onto ships or lorries in order that it might be delivered by those to whom we expressed our gratitude a moment ago. We pray for those who drove those lorries and sailed those ships, pray for their families, their friends and their neighbours. We remember those who grew this food in the first place in distant lands, the ones who picked and harvested it, their families, their children, those who teach their children, and the head teachers of the schools that those children attend. We thank you for the food that the children in those schools eat, those who prepare and cook it, and the good folk who deliver it to the school in order that it might be cooked. We want to thank you for the governments of the countries in which those schools are located, for those who govern, for all whom they love, and all who love them, for the food they eat and, of course, for those who prepare and cook it. We remember – waiter, this food's almost cold, who's responsible for that?

Three

Entry into the outrageous, frightening, funny no-man's land of true Christian commitment

Hold your nerve

Do you get frightened? I do. In the world of true spiritual involvement, it is almost certain to happen. Here are two examples of situations where I have experienced profound fear. One is easy to understand, the other is a bit weird, but probably more significant. The first is connected with a trip to Canada in the autumn of 2009. Bridget and I had moved to Yorkshire in the August of that year, and from the day we arrived there was a succession of problems to be endured or overcome, particularly in connection with close family. We were more convinced about being in the right place than at any other time in our lives, and it became a habit for one of us to murmur, 'Hold your nerve', whenever these grinding difficulties arose. We Christians get a bit carried away with the cosy notion that all catastrophes are evidence that we are on the right track, and therefore under continual attack from the devil, but towards the end of the year this over-used argument acquired a chilling relevance.

Bridget was driving me along the M25 to catch my flight to Toronto at Heathrow Airport. We had already decided that, because of harrowing family problems, Bridget would have to cancel her involvement in this tour, but as we neared the Heathrow turn-off something else happened.

I gather that most major accidents on motorways are caused by East European lorries that are not equipped with mirrors allowing their drivers to see cars overtaking them in an adjacent lane. That is what happened to us. One sickeningly massive impact on the rear side of our car slewed us round, followed by three more crunching blows on the passenger door as the huge lorry pile-drove us into the metal railings at the side of the motorway.

Silence fell. I looked at Bridget. She appeared to be okay. She looked at me. As far as I could tell, I was physically unharmed as well. I don't remember saying anything at this point, but Bridget tells me that I said three words.

'Hold your nerve.'

The car was written off and we were very shaken, but by God's grace we did hold our nerve. I caught a plane to Canada the next day, and we remained in the place to which we were called.

The second experience of fear is more recent, but has a close connection with the first.

Unable to sleep one night, I quietly left my bed and moved to the window. It was dark, and I mean *dark*. Our part of the Yorkshire Dales is officially designated one of the 'darkest' spots in the British Isles. On this particular night heavy cloud blanketed the stars and it was pitch-black outside. Occasional calls and cries and wild screams echoed from the merciless world of woodland and meadow that surrounds our house. None of that bothered me. A part of my strange soul has always been drawn to the sweetness of the night.

No, the thing that caused a shadow of dread to sink like a stone through my being was a renewed awareness that being a Christian, following Jesus, entering a world that is only as safe in worldly terms as God allows it to be, is very, very frightening. There is a final step that has to be taken, an act of assent inviting a quality of darkness that can only be dispelled by journeying through this dense cloud in search of a unique and uniquely revealing light. No Easter Day without a Good Friday. It scares me to death sometimes. That night it terrified me. It still does, but I don't think I can go backwards, and I would find it very tedious to stand still. It could be quite a journey. I must hold my nerve. I pray that you will as well.

Helpers rather than consumers

Part of that journey for us has involved new and unexpected destinations over the last ten years. Bridget and I have been presented with a wonderful gift. God has allowed us to have a small but practical role in the work of aid agencies around the world. We have walked through the streets of Bangladeshi slums, observed work being done with AIDS sufferers in Africa, and, more recently, made trips to South and Central America to visit projects supported by Toybox, the British street child charity.

Why is this gift so welcome to us? Well, rather pathetically I suppose, although our tasks are certainly humble by comparison with those continually performed by men and women at the sharp end of these wonderful enterprises, at least we have been given a reasonably defined job to do. We go there, we make notes about everything we see, then we come back and write books about our travels, or show films and photographs of people and places we have visited. Generally, we are able to share our continually refreshed passion for bringing relief to those who suffer poverty, neglect and cruelty around the world. I hope we help a bit. We do try.

But let's not talk nonsense about this. My wife and I are as capable of indulgence and selfishness as the next struggling pair of Christians. The fact is, though, that we always did want to be helpers rather than consumers in the Body of Christ, and having such clearly shaped responsibilities makes it that much easier. However, as we all know, even if we don't want to face it, our responsibilities rarely come in neatly wrapped packages, and most of them are located outside, not inside, the immediate church environment. Not only that, but many of these 'jobs from God' are less than spectacular in nature. People are sometimes disappointed with revival because it boils down to visiting the housebound elderly lady down the road twice a week instead of once. Tough. This is the Jesus way. Small, and beautifully formed. It may not fit in with the world (or large sections of the church, I'm afraid) but it is where the Holy Spirit is, and if we want to be true to our Master, we had better be there as well.

The demands of Jesus on our lives seem to be overwhelming. How can we cope with this? What makes it worthwhile to press on and do the stuff that crops up all the time? Can 'church' be bad for Christians? What are the causes of spiritual constipation? If Jesus came back in the flesh and visited my town or city, where would he spend most of his time? Don't expect me to answer all these questions. I'm a searcher like you. If you ever meet me in the street, come over and compare notes. Here's a thought, though.

Ever since our first trip to Bangladesh with World Vision, there has been a realisation or a conclusion I reached that I have never managed to express very clearly. It reminds me of a little poem I wrote after reading Constantine Fitzgibbon's biography of Dylan Thomas. Somehow I had lost a little vision that had been important to me.

I used to know what poetry is for
I have forgotten
Something to do with how to be
Or how to feel
It meant so much
The words remain
But the knowledge has gone
Like a poem that never really worked

My Bangladesh conclusion, reinforced when we travelled to Zambia to look at work with AIDS, is to do with the way in which God does or does not intervene in the world. In the slums of Dhaka, the capital of Bangladesh, we saw little girls being rescued from the imminent prospect of prostitution, families helped to climb out of poverty, and whole communities provided with clean water, health-care and education. We were deeply impressed by the work that was being done to assist and constructively educate Zambian people of all ages in issues connected with the appalling, family-rending effects of HIV/AIDS. In recent years we have travelled to Central and South America to see the work done by the charity Toybox in supporting organisations involved with preventive and residential work among street children. Lots of wonderful projects devised and supported by committed workers who focus on the task of expressing the love of God through practical service.

All that is more than fine, but an abiding memory is the moment when Bridget and I sat on some funny old chairs outside a tumbledown shack in a Zambian village, waiting for a lady called Rois who was suffering from full-blown AIDS to be helped out of her home to meet us. She was very sick indeed, and the prognosis was grim. There were no expensive retro-viral drugs available. Rois would probably be dead within a couple of weeks, leaving two children without parents. She had only three things to hope for. She hoped that heaven would offer her something better than she had known on earth; that the good ladies from World Vision and other agencies would continue to visit her with comfort and simple medicines until her death; and that someone would look after her children after she had gone.

They sat her down on an old maize sack on the dusty yellow earth that sunny morning, and we all looked at each other. A reflux of panic rose suddenly into my throat, threatening to physically choke me. There was something wrong here, something that didn't fit, something that denied one whole dimension of my experience. It was a sense of radical unease that had begun during our trip to Bangladesh, and had grown in intensity ever since. Let me see if I can express it clearly for once.

In the countries that we have visited on behalf of World Vision and Toybox, there are people of all ages suffering from extreme poverty, illness and neglect. In the worst of these situations, as far as we can see, God is not doing anything for these people unless it happens through his followers, or through those who represent other organisations than Christian ones. Don't misunderstand me. I believe in miracles. I always have done. But God is not preventing little girls from dying in heartbreaking circumstances on the streets of the slums. There is no evidence of manna falling from heaven to feed starving children, no waves of divine healing rolling through the AIDS-infested villages that we have visited. As Mother Teresa so succinctly expressed it, in the vast majority of cases, the only hands that God has are our hands.

Meanwhile, in rich, comfortable countries like ours, there are Bible studies and prayer meetings and worship sessions, in which followers of Jesus celebrate the fact that God is helping with mortgage payments, healing illnesses, paying for cars, arranging marriages, tailoring bespoke coincidences and saving parking spaces outside supermarkets for his privileged servants. It appears that, in these parts of the world, God speaks to people, listens to people, caters for people and generally mops up after people.

Does he? Can these two contrasting worlds possibly exist on the same planet? Has God decided to give up on losers and concentrate on those who have made something of themselves? Extremely unlikely I would say. But what do I know?

All I do know for sure is that as I sat opposite Rois, silently asking God to tell me where I could plug in my faith in this place that appeared to have no power source, a verse from James chapter 1 came into my mind: 'Religion that God our Father accepts as pure and faultless is this: to look after orphans and widows in their distress and to keep oneself from being polluted by the world.'

Rois had almost nothing. How much would you or I have if all our material comforts were swept away? Which world do we want to inhabit? The one where God is, or some other, more entertaining sphere?

In this connection, it's always interesting to discover the sorts of things that shock Christians. The American speaker and writer Tony Campolo famously used a swear word at a Christian festival, and then challenged his audience to ask themselves if they were more shocked by one swear word than the fact that millions of people are dying of starvation, malaria and AIDS in the Two-Thirds World. Last year at harvest time our local vicar, Peter Yorkstone, pointed out that harvest means different things to different people all over the world. Given my ingrained tendency to stretch an interesting or amusing idea out to the point where it snaps, it was almost inevitable that I would produce something along the following lines. The last verse before the chorus describes the meagre harvest available to children in Central and South America, and in other equally impoverished parts of the world.

Harvest

We plough the fields and scatter the good seed on the land
But it is fed and watered by God's almighty hand

We raise our lambs for slaughter before they're old and coarse
And then we cut the best bits off and eat them with mint sauce

We shoot the seals and scatter their entrails on the ice
The coats we make up from their furs are very warm and nice

We hunt for bits of plastic upon the garbage heap
And twice a week we sell enough to eat before we sleep

All good gifts around us are sent at heaven's behest
Then thank the Lord, O thank the Lord, we've got more than
the rest.

The body beautiful

Yes, we certainly need to be more generous with our concern and our cash, but having said that, there are positive movements in the Christian community in countries like ours. For instance, churches get together much more than they used to. That is certainly true in the United Kingdom, where inter-church initiatives have become quite common in our villages, towns and cities. I suppose a cynic might see this as the product of a panic-stricken realisation that miniscule groups of worshippers have to be combined in order to make up one decent-sized congregation, but I think there is more to it. One of the unexpected advantages of falling attendances in our churches is that, in many cases, the people we are left with have a genuine concern for their faith in general and Jesus in particular.

Yes, all right, you don't have to remind me that there are exceptions to both of these optimistic assessments. I still hear about churches whose members are convinced that they have happened upon the one true way to heaven and cannot bear the thought of besmirching their purity by connection with outsiders. And yes, there are certainly congregational remnants who would hang on to their habitual seats, their routine and their denominational preferences, even if Jesus himself were to appear and ask them to do something slightly different. Nevertheless, I remain hopeful. The signs are good.

The cautionary word that I would offer (with the profound humility that characterises my every utterance) is that unity between Christians cannot successfully be imposed by leaders, unless their followers are properly informed and genuinely willing to have a go at pursuing a vision that may take them adventuring into a world beyond the secure little islands of their personal preference.

Is it okay to have different patterns and ways of worship? How can it be that Christians develop priorities that put 'the way we do things' near the top of the list, and Jesus somewhere down on the same level as chair arranging and refreshments? What could possibly help this situation? One more question. What would church unity look like at its best?

I guess, in the end, that this and other issues of forward movement in the church must be a matter of establishing priorities. The other evening I attended a meeting of something called the Deanery Synod at a local Anglican church. I have no intention of explaining what this means, not least because I have no idea. Suffice to say that it involves members of clergy and lay people from local churches in the area. When I leaned over to ask a lady what it was all about her reply was dryly expressed, to say the least.

'A Deanery Synod,' she said, placing her hand beside her mouth so that no-one else could hear, 'is a collection of Anglicans sitting around, waiting to go home.'

An exaggeration – surely? I'm an Anglican, and I'm incredibly lively and alert. You should see me!

My serious question is this. When God looks at his church, especially in this part of the world, does he see a load of Christians sitting around, waiting to go home? In both world wars in the last century there were examples of amazing bravery and devotion to duty among chaplains associated with the armed services. These were people who were not content to simply stay behind the lines and preach. They were determined to share the problems and hardships of men who lived in the midst of mud and bullets and the extreme probability of death. Some, like Geoffrey Studdert Kennedy, the famous World War 1 chaplain, were decorated for outstanding acts of bravery and heroism carried out in the hell that was called no-man's-land.

And that, if you don't mind me saying so, is where we Christians should be. It will mean different things for each one of us, and denominational unity may well be the least of these, but if we think we are fulfilling our responsibilities by sitting around behind the lines waiting to go home, we had better think again. There are some questions that are well worth asking.

What is no-man's-land for me? Which part of my comfort zone might I have to vacate in order to follow Jesus into places where I can make a difference? What were Elijah's experiences in the thick of spiritual battle? You can read about him in 1 Kings if you want to. It might put you off Christian service altogether. On the other hand . . .

Is it fear or inertia or something else that stands in the way of sacrificial service to God?

Paul

One piece of good news is that there can be unexpected rewards for those who take the fearful step into no-man's-land. I am approaching my sixty-third birthday as I write, and my friend Paul Taphouse is a year younger than me. He is one of my best friends in the world. Bridget and I love him dearly. I wrote quite a lot about my friendship with Paul in a book called *Jesus – Safe Tender Extreme*,[1] published a few years ago. He lives in a home for men and women with learning difficulties and has a sweet, sweet nature. About twenty-five years ago I very, very nervously obeyed a call from God to become Paul's friend. It took me an awful long time to get on with what I was being asked to do. I was such a coward. When I did finally give in, I was presented with a gift that was valuable beyond anything I could imagine. Paul's friendship has wonderfully enriched our lives. I do hope you have the chance to read about that first encounter if you get the chance.

Paul is a poet and a musician, and one of the things he and I have enjoyed most over the years is writing poetry together. Here is one of our joint efforts, and if you were to ask me what it is about, I would have to reply that I am not sure. Actually, I haven't the faintest idea. It doesn't matter. It came from somewhere in both of us and, however strange, there is an interesting, sad dankness about the words, and it means whatever it means.

Pan-pipes

God, I can't remember what the pan-pipes mean
Took a turning miles back along a path I'd never seen
Leaves and grasses, trees and bushes just as green
But my walk wound through the darkness of a deep ravine
Down in hopeless places where the dying saplings lean
And I am just as sad and sober as I've ever been
I hear the pan-pipes but I can't remember what they mean

Time to see the blue bits

Twenty years ago, one of the southern universities did some research into crucial aspects of counselling technique. I remember reading that they finally identified three main features as essential aspects of this kind of work. First of all, they decided, the good counsellor must be willing to enter into their client's world. Secondly, they must not judge or condemn their client's behaviour. And thirdly, they must demonstrate that they value their client. I recall thinking when I read these findings that the researchers could have saved themselves a lot of trouble by dipping into the New Testament and reading about Jesus, the mighty Counsellor, who entered into our world, not to condemn us, but to show, by giving his life on the cross, how highly we are valued. Reflecting this generous-hearted approach to those we encounter seems to me an inescapable requirement if we truly want to live in and be involved with the world inhabited by the Holy Spirit.

In this connection I would like to tell you a little story or parable, a memory of one of the most charming, fascinating things I ever saw.

My friend Michael lived with his wife and son in one half of a cottage on the edge of a forest in a remote part of the west country. Michael was an art dealer, a well-spoken, highly cultured man who loved books and sculpture and poetry. His house was a treasure chest of antiques, prints and original paintings, one of those rare homes where it is difficult to find any item, however trivial, that is cheap or garish or purchased without critical consideration. There was, however, nothing precious or affected about the way Michael displayed his possessions. The little Victorian cottage was pleasantly messy and unmanicured, a refreshingly unthreatening situation for people like me who find domestic perfection awe-inspiring but deeply worrying. I loved being in Michael's house, and I loved Michael. He was one of those human beings who inspire you to rise from what you dismally suspect you probably are, to become something you might be if you were ever to give yourself half a chance.

Next door to Michael lived Bill, a man whose life was mostly about wood. He was employed by the local estate owners to control forest growth, cut and sell timber and generally take responsibility for the forest environment. Bill was tall, bony and physically strong, a cheerful, consistently honest and straightforward man, who, as far as I could tell, was untutored and uninterested in any aspect of the arts. I had been into his sitting-room once or twice. It was unfussily functional and unornamented, a space where, at the end of a tiring day, you could eat your supper or read the paper or watch a bit of television before going to bed. Bill's was a rhythmic, simple life.

Michael and Bill lived on these two very different if immediately adjacent little planets, but they had a very amiable relationship. Michael's gift for making others feel better about themselves was as effective with his neighbour as it was with everyone else. Bill clearly admired Michael enormously and seemed to regard the inside of the next-door house as a sort of cultural Tardis. How could such an abundance of esoteric knowledge and understanding be contained within a space no larger than his own living-room?

During one of my all too infrequent visits to Michael's cottage there was a knock on the door as we drank coffee together.

'That'll be Bill,' said Michael, lowering his mug, 'time to see the blue bits. Come and have a look.'

Puzzling.

A few seconds later we were standing in Bill's living-room, surveying a large rectangular sheet of cardboard balanced on a makeshift easel near the window. Next to it, on the rough, grainy table that Bill used for his meals, there were five or six little plastic pots of paint and a jam jar half filled with water. A cheap paintbrush, its head tinged with bright green, rested on a shallow dish. Bill gestured proprietorially in the direction of the easel.

'I've finished all the green,' he said with gruff pride to Michael, 'What do you think?'

It was quite wonderful to see. Supporting an elbow with the back of one hand, and stroking his chin reflectively with the other, Michael, who knew as much about all aspects of art as anyone I've ever met, drew his head back, narrowed his eyes, and studied the latest work done by Bill on one of the pre-printed sheets from his painting by numbers set. It was as though Da Vinci had sought reassurance regarding his depiction of La Giaconda's smile.

'Amazingly accurate,' said Michael, shaking his head admiringly, 'I don't know how you manage to stay so neatly inside the lines. Was that tricky?'

'Not too bad,' replied Bill, 'you 'ave to – you know – really concentrate.'

'Yep, yep, I can see that, and so – now, what comes next? Would it be the blue, or does it make more sense to leave that, seeing as it's mainly sky?'

'They tell you the order to do it in,' explained Bill earnestly. He picked up a printed sheet from the table and studied it for a moment. 'Brown's next, then yellow. D'you want to 'ave a look?'

'I'd *love* to,' said Michael animatedly. He reached out a hand to take the sheet. 'Aah, right, I get you. Now, let's just go through this . . .'

It was typical of Michael that we never discussed this exquisite encounter after leaving Bill's house. It would have been treacherous, and my friend was never that. For me it was a unique experience, filled with eager trust and fragility and imminent danger and love. I never forgot it.

Blessed are the seafarers

The kind of sensitivity demonstrated by Michael is occasionally and rather surprisingly demonstrated by organisations.

A few years ago a very close friend of mine from college days called Mark Warner took up a post with The Sailors' Society, an organisation that began in the nineteenth century after a blessedly sane Christian passed a church bearing the sign: No Sailors or Prostitutes. Talk about standing the gospel on its head. Nowadays, The Sailors' Society provides a personal lifeline for seafarers not only on board ship, but also when they step ashore. The Society's publicity states that it exists to enrich and enhance the well-being of seafarers in port through its Port Chaplains and centres, seafarers being offered practical help and welfare, spiritual support, financial assistance and family liaison. And we discovered that this claim is justified. Port Chaplains visit thousands of ships during the year and are often the first to notice when all is not well on board. They reach out to crew members of all ranks, with no regard to faith, denomination, ethnic background or nationality, offering a friendly presence, and unconditionally greeting seafarers wherever they meet them.

Over the last couple of years, Bridget and I have been pleased and privileged to have opportunities to support

The Sailors' Society in a number of ways. As with many very focussed charities, it is easy for the excellent, heart-warming things they do to be invisible to the general public. After asking a lot of questions about a world and a lifestyle that were totally alien to me, I did my best to encapsulate the experience of isolation and loneliness that seafarers can experience.

Isolation

I see them in the morning when I wake
In that split second just before my eyelids part
I see them all so clearly
Hear them calling me from sad, sweet dreams
My people. My house. My street. My sky. My world
Warmer than my bed, warmer than a fire, how they shine
Inwardly my arms stretch out to them in foolish, yearning
    hope
'This time, dear God,' I pray through tiny cracks in each
    unsullied dawn
'Allow it to be so. Allow it to be real.'
But then the voices come, the sounds that make no sense to
    me
The echoes of an unfamiliar song
The thud and crash and creak of things that must be done
The ever-present limits of this crunching space
And yes, there are the people
Yes, there is an endless, overarching sky
And yes, there is a place, a place to be
Although it is not, never will be mine
All day I nurse the prospect of the night
Dreaming dreams that lift my lonely heart
And fly me to the gently coloured world where I belong

Woolly hats

Bridget and I love our very marginal involvement with Christian organisations like these, the ones that no-one hears much about. As the years go by we become more and more convinced that many of the most effective initiatives happen in small, not very visible ways. Jesus meets lonely, bewildered seafarers through the kindness and practical assistance of men and women who are paid very little and care very much: Christian involvement at its best. We have done a handful of fundraising events for The Sailors' Society and they were great fun, but it was a special joy to be asked to write the following piece as a contribution to their centenary celebrations. Incidentally, the reference to woolly hats is not as trivial as it might sound. Hundreds of people have knitted these head warmers for seafarers who are not accustomed to cold climates, and they are much appreciated. During the 'Woolly Hat Tour' Bridget and I actually wore them from time to time. Bridget looked fine, but I had the appearance of a demented gnome. Greater love hath no man . . .

Blessed are

Blessed are those whose heads are uncovered in cold climates and upon cold seas, for they shall receive woolly hats. And blessed are those who create the woolly hats by the toil of their hands, for they shall be called servants of the most High.

Blessed are those who worry and grieve for those they love who are impossibly far away, for they shall be comforted and connected. And blessed are those who comfort and connect them, for they shall see the light of relief where once there was darkness and fear.

Blessed are those who need to see a friendly face and gentle eyes, for they shall be warmed by the smiling grace of God. And blessed are those who bring the kindness of heaven to the hearts of the lost, for they shall be called children of the light.

Blessed are those who know the terror of storms, for they shall see Jesus at peace in the midst of confusion. And blessed are those who show the face of the serene Jesus to those who are lost and bewildered, for they shall see the mysterious power of God.

Blessed are those who are bullied and cheated and underpaid and used and manipulated, for they shall be represented and made safe by the strong arms of caring and careful support. And blessed are those who support the mistreated, for they shall receive mercy instead of justice.

Blessed are those who never hear their own language in a strange land, for they shall be taught the language of love. And blessed are those who speak the language of love to those who are lonely, for they shall be the messengers of God.

Blessed are those who have nowhere to go and nothing to do when work has ended, for they shall be given places to visit and books to read and games to play and a community to be part of. And blessed are those who make all these things available to weary travellers, for they, in their turn, shall be refreshed.

Blessed are you when nights are long and days are hard and uncertainty reigns and you eat alone and dream of home and nobody seems to understand, for God will send a friend to meet your needs and serve you well. And blessed are you who bless and serve and protect with no thought of reward, for you are the hands and feet of the Saviour.

Blessings on the sailors.
Blessings on those who serve them.
Blessed be the name of Jesus.

The child who threw her cloak in front of Jesus

I suspect that people are getting a bit tired of hearing me say that God has just as many problems with principles as he does with sin. People use all sorts of ploys to avoid the risk of stepping out into areas and types of behaviour that are new and contradictory as far as they are concerned. Jesus only ever did what he saw his Father doing, and sometimes it looked pretty bizarre. Chucking tables around, cursing fig trees, insulting dignitaries, healing on the Sabbath? He was a publicist's nightmare. Do you really want to follow him?

Here is a child who learned this very important lesson on the very first Palm Sunday, and probably never forgot it.

Dear Grandmother,

How are you? How is Grandfather? Please give him
my love. Mother and father send their love as well.
Mother says I am to write to you with my news. My
biggest news is that I have decided I do not want to be a
girl. It is not fair for girls. We have to grow up to be
women, and women have no fun. Men are not that nice,
but if I had been a boy who became a man, I would have
turned into a man who was more like a woman who is
allowed to be a man but still be like a woman. No-one
even asked me what I wanted to be. Too late now.

My second biggest news is something that happened to
me that I have made a riddle out of. Grandfather told me
about riddles. Here is mine. What is naughty and good as
well? The answer is something I did yesterday when I
went with mother to see the teacher called Jesus. Mother
likes Jesus. She says he is the most important person in the
world, but as father says she does get a bit carried away.

Anyway, she took me to see him coming into
Jerusalem, and he came riding towards us on a sweet little colt with a white patch on the side of its nose (a bit
small for him, actually). Such a funny thing happened to
me when I saw his face. It was a whooshing and a rushing like a whooshing, rushing river of warm water trying
to burst out of my chest and my head. I wanted to cheer
and shout and throw my cloak on the ground in front of
Jesus. I didn't because mother always says it is naughty to
tear my clothes and make them dirty. But then, when I
told her about the warm water and wanting to throw my
cloak down and everything, she said I must do it, and we
both ended up cheering and shouting until our throats
were sore. Lots of people did. It was great!

When can something you do be naughty and good as
well? When it is for Jesus.

Lost in transit

A trivial footnote to this section. As mentioned earlier, Bridget and I have travelled to distant lands, not only in support of charities and aid agencies, but also to tour or speak at conferences and events all over the world, often accompanied by our children. Those who know me well are sometimes sceptical about my ability to organise myself sufficiently to actually turn up at the correct obscure destination on the appropriate date. Fortunately, Bridget is very efficient when it comes to the business of planning travel. So far I think we have arrived safely on every occasion, but I do have to admit that when I recently assembled a catalogue of items lost over the last couple of decades it made alarming reading. We really have managed to lose or nearly lose an astonishing variety of things. Let me share my list with you.

We have littered six continents with sunglasses, cameras, odd socks, cricket bats, essential documents, keys, books, presents for people back home, underwear left in hotel drawers (oh, the ignominy of it!), combs, bags, sweatshirts and one much loved teddy bear called Gregory. Don't worry, this caused such trauma for our daughter that we went to endless, highly complicated and expensive trouble to get him posted back home from Sydney.

We have *nearly* lost: all our money to thieves in Spain, and, during the same holiday, to another set of thieves in Dover. In both cases our money had actually been stolen, but we knew who had taken it immediately and the sheer ingenious bolshiness of the entire Plass clan seemed to persuade both sets of bewildered criminals that the option of giving the money back was easily preferable to keeping it.

I lost half of one of my earlobes in New Zealand when we went fishing and my son Joe cast a spoon (large metal object with barbs attached to it) and caught my ear. It was like being hit in the side of the head by a brick. I then had to go to the local surgery wearing the spoon like a bizarre earring to have it removed. My arrival certainly brightened a dull day for the medical staff. I don't think there was a single person who didn't find my innovative jewellery screamingly funny.

I thought I had lost my daughter forever when she disappeared under the water when our boat overturned in a river in Denmark. Eventually she turned up, bobbing about in the water under the overturned boat. Her first words at this point were, 'I knew I'd be all right, Daddy, because you were here.' By no means necessarily true, but a wonderful Christian parable.

We came close to losing hope on the desolate border between Zambia and the Congo, where lorry drivers are stranded for weeks while endless bureaucracy grinds its way to a conclusion. This geographical and social no-man's-land is the place where young sex-workers come looking for customers and find plenty of them among bored drivers who are far from home. For many of these girls it is the only source of income that they are likely to find.

'Can we come and work in your house in England?' they asked us, obviously picturing a huge baronial mansion awash with servants.

World Vision do some wonderful, quiet work with these lovely girls, and also with the drivers, who are just as needy in their own way.

What else? We very nearly lost our voices when the sound failed in Auckland Cathedral and we had to shout our gentle, loving message to the masses. Unfortunately the masses were terminally distracted by the work going on behind us as technicians struggled to remedy the sound problem, so the whole event was a bit of a disaster.

We have definitely lost: the will to live in Los Angeles airport (you will too if you go there), most of several meals in Bolivia, every single bit of luggage on our very first trip to Australia, height far too rapidly in a plane landing in snow and fog in Canada, and our dignity in Peru.

The Peru thing. I should explain that all of the Toybox team were suffering from diarrhoea when we arrived in Lima, and when we went to a chemist to ask for medicine, the pharmacist showed us something akin to a paint-chart featuring colours that ranged from bright yellow to dark brown. Which of these corresponded in colour to the major symptom of our condition? That was what she wanted to know. Jolly, eh?

We lost our confidence in America, all our souvenirs to corrupt customs officers in Azerbaijan, weight in Sweden and Switzerland (as we couldn't afford to eat), our way for several dismal hours in Holland, which has a most odd system of signposting, our cool in traffic jams in Bangladesh, our belief in marriage as an institution in quite a lot of places, and our hearts to thousands of children we have seen and met all over the world.

But – we have never lost our passports! Not yet.

Four

Unauthorised fire

Priorities

When I sat down to think about priorities for this book I very soon realised that the issue of unauthorised fire must come very near the top of the list. Here is something well worth fighting for. Our Christian *War of the Worlds* hots up when we face the need to defend an exclusive commitment to the genuine power and will of God against human inventions, religious excesses, tired patterns and the bullying disguised as spiritual authority that is often motivated by lust for power. The phrase 'unauthorised fire' comes from the Old Testament.

At the foot of Mount Sinai

When I was asked to write some Bible notes on Leviticus for the Bible Reading Fellowship a few years ago I was not terribly excited, but I couldn't help getting inter-ested as I began to explore this very complex and intense piece of work. It is filled with a sort of urgent drive towards making sure that every tiny detail needed to establish a right relationship between God and his people has not been omitted.

I became particularly interested in the section that describes the swift and apparently merciless execution of Aaron's two sons when, as you will see, they went a flame too far. Their crime was a use of fire that was not authorised by God. Aaron must have been devastated. 'False fire' also crops up in the profoundly challenging book of Malachi, if you care to look it up. These things set me thinking about unauthorised fire as a metaphor for unacceptable religious practices in our own age. But before we think about those, let's remember those incredibly dramatic moments in the desert at the foot of Mount Sinai all those years ago.

Washed and wrapped for business: Leviticus 8:5–9

> Moses said to the assembly, 'This is what the Lord has commanded to be done.'
> Then Moses brought Aaron and his sons forward and washed them with water. He put the tunic on Aaron, tied the sash around him, clothed him with the robe and put the ephod on him. He also tied the ephod to him by its skilfully woven waistband; so it was fastened on him. He placed the breast piece on him and put the Urim and Thummim in the breast piece. Then he placed the turban on Aaron's head and set the gold plate, the sacred diadem, on the front of it, as the Lord commanded Moses.

This really is extraordinary, isn't it? It reminds me of one of James Herriot's stories of life as a country vet in Yorkshire. The young Herriot was persuaded by a grizzled old veterinary practitioner to wear a ridiculously confining rubber calving suit and cap at a local farm. To the amusement of onlookers, it transpired that the role of this amazingly attired person was simply to pass a pessary to the senior vet.

Here is Aaron dressed up like a cross between Widow Twanky and Darth Vader. And this was only the beginning. After the sons had been washed and Aaron had donned his complicated gear, they all had to be marked with sacrificial blood on their right ears, hands and toes. Then they were sprinkled, robes and all, with oil and blood. Aaron must have felt like echoing the words spoken so often by Oliver Hardy to Stan Laurel: 'Another fine mess you've got me into!'

Seriously, why was all this dressing up and sprinkling and washing so important? Perhaps it has something to do with the need for Aaron and his sons to be totally immersed, absorbed and bound up in the important task that lay before them. Human beings are so fickle and distractible. The complexity of ceremonial detail was like a net, holding them fast until the job was done, and done properly.

We don't have to do all that fiddling around nowadays, but how much of ourselves do we voluntarily throw into the tasks that God gives us? Freedom feels like hard work sometimes.

Authorised fire: Leviticus 9:22–24

Then Aaron lifted his hands towards the people and blessed them. And having sacrificed the sin offering, the burnt offering and the fellowship offering, he stepped down.

Moses and Aaron then went into the tent of meeting. When they came out they blessed the people; and the glory of the Lord appeared to all the people. Fire came out from the presence of the Lord and consumed the burnt offering and the fat portions on the altar. And when all the people saw it, they shouted for joy and fell facedown.

Here we find ourselves at the end of the long and complicated process involved in the ordination of Aaron and his sons as priests. Bulls, goats, rams, and calves have been prepared and offered, all in a meticulously ceremonial fashion, in order to atone for the sins of the new priests and the whole nation of Israel. God has promised that if all is done well, he will appear to them and show his glory. Now the moment has come. Suddenly, as Moses and Aaron come out of the tent of meeting and bless the people, supernatural fire roars into life, consuming the sacrifices and filling the people with a rich, exhilarating mixture of joy and terror.

Isn't it good when God turns up? Of course he's there all the time, but you know what I mean. When times have been hard, and the road has been rough, and you've tried not very successfully to do the right and obedient thing, and you're just about ready to give up, isn't it fantastic when the authentic fire of God blazes into your life? It turns all that you offer to ashes, but leaves you quivering with relief and joy because he has come, and heaven has once more swept reassuringly across the earth, and everything is all right.

Doesn't happen often, does it? Not really. Why not? I wonder if it is connected with the casual inconsistency with which we conduct our spiritual journeys. I remember John Wimber, who obediently preached healing for a year during which nobody was healed, and then saw the power of God working in the bodies of countless people. I have a deep yearning to see the fire of God. I'm just not sure if I can keep my feet firmly on a path that seems very wearisome at times.

Unauthorised fire: Leviticus 10:1–5

> Aaron's sons Nadab and Abihu took their censers, put fire in them and added incense; and they offered unauthorized fire before the Lord, contrary to his command. So fire came out from the presence of the Lord and consumed them, and they died before the Lord. Moses then said to Aaron, This is what the Lord spoke of when he said, 'Among those who approach me I will be proved holy; in the sight of all the people I will be honoured.'
>
> Aaron remained silent.
>
> Moses summoned Mishael and Elzaphan, sons of Aaron's uncle Uzziel, and said to them, 'Come here; carry your cousins outside the camp, away from the front of the sanctuary.' So they came and carried them, still in their tunics, outside the camp, as Moses ordered.

Oh, dear.

As I have already pointed out, in the opening chapter of Malachi God rebukes his priests for offering 'false fire' at the altar. When will we learn that God never, never, never appreciates the fabricated spirituality of those who get carried away by purely human excitement and ambition?

What a sad story this is. The Bible surprises me sometimes with a sentence so poignantly vivid that it brings tears to my eyes. An example appears in Matthew 14. When Jesus heard about the death of his cousin John, he 'withdrew by boat privately to a solitary place'. Of course, the crowds soon found him. Jesus never had much time for himself.

'Aaron remained silent.'

Overwhelmed by grief at the death of his sons, what else can he do? There's nothing to say. Nahab and Abihu got it wrong. They tried to make God happen, and God didn't like it. How sad to learn that they were carried off 'still in their tunics', colourful symbols of a future that had looked so bright and successful.

Talk about a spiritual boot camp, eh? What a tough course: no compromise, no second chances. My way or the highway, thus (more or less) saith the Lord. Clearly there was a need for absolute purity in the priesthood, and I expect God knew what he was doing. He usually does.

However we react to this sorry tale, one lesson is clear. Don't try to make God happen. He doesn't like it. It won't work. The fire has to come from him.

Beware the golden calf

That's what happened in that far off age, but if any of us really believes that unauthorised fire is limited to Old Testament days, we had better think again. There's plenty of it about, and it appears for a number of reasons. Let's look at one or two of them.

One of the most common grows out of a relatively innocent desire to experience closeness with a God who doesn't seem to turn up in the ways that we have been taught to expect. Perhaps if we beef up the Sunday service with lots of dramatic visuals and flashing lights and extravagant special effects and fabricated voices from heaven, we will convince ourselves and everyone else that God himself must be in the middle of it all somewhere. Maybe if the choir could reach new heights of excellence and the sound system were to be replaced with gear that is absolutely state of the art, the Holy Spirit might be tempted to inhabit the space we have created.

Nothing wrong with any of these things in themselves, of course, but if they are intended to create a golden calf that might be mistaken for God, then we are almost certainly wasting our time.

Much less innocent are those individuals who have experienced the intoxicating flavour of power on their tongues and want a lot more of the same. Many of our brothers and sisters in the body of Christ are dangerously vulnerable to these wolves in sheep's clothing. When your heart is yearning like a lost lamb to find a shepherd who can be trusted, it is easy to be seduced by a voice that sounds confident or a manner that seems assured. My wife and I have met and ministered to far too many of these victims of bullying and cruel domination. God doesn't behave like that. He may be tough, but he's also nice, and he never bullies.

The things that God actually does are the only true influences for good. Fakes are at best a waste of time, and at worst seriously damaging to those who are fooled by them. I recall, for instance, a German friend telling me that as a young man he had been told by someone who claimed to have a prophetic gift that he was homosexual. The effect of this idiotic pronouncement was catastrophic. My friend was at an age and in a frame of mind where he believed that the things said to him by older, more experienced Christians must be from God. It is not an exaggeration to say that his life was crippled by that carelessly delivered statement. Years later he met the man who had injured him so thoughtlessly and asked how he felt about what he had done. The 'prophet' was unrepentant. 'Ah well,' he said, 'we were always taught that it's best to just speak these things out if they came into our heads. We wouldn't want to miss the things that are from God because we're worrying about the things that aren't, would we?'

I would like to go on record as saying that I have rarely heard such a load of unsorted garbage. True prophecy is a jewel without price, but we should never, never, never to the power of eternity, say the kind of intrusive and potentially damaging things that my friend had to endure, unless we have taken time to pray and consult with someone who is wiser than us – not too difficult in my case. I would also add that these things don't always have to be labelled as prophecy when they are expressed, nor do they have to be spoken out in ponderous biblical language. If they are from God, they will find a home, and if they are not, these precautions offer a built-in possibility of damage limitation.

An example? A friend of mine was sitting next to a man he knew in a church service down in Devon one day. His neighbour was laughing at something that had been said at the front. My friend found a sentence forming in his mind and believed that it was for the man next to him. Leaning across, he whispered, 'Do you believe all this stuff?' In the middle of his laughter this fellow began to cry, and quite a chunk of the rest of the day was spent in talking and praying about the source of these tears. Prophecy? Probably, but it in a way didn't really matter, did it?

Yes, of course there are times when a communication from God has to be spoken out boldly and immediately, but we had better be extremely careful if there is any chance that our message could potentially have a negative effect.

I wonder what experiences you have had of unauthorised fire? There are so many different ways in which this can happen. I would be most interested to hear how you got burned, as long as the telling is not too painful. I sincerely hope you have also known instances of twenty-four

carat God-generated events or happenings, as I have on a
few occasions. This subject generates so many questions.
How can we tell the difference between the real thing and
false fire? Why doesn't God make it easier? Certainly, the
world of divinely authorised fire may be a little bewilder-
ing at times. This is inevitable when real life is happening
(join Paul in his colourful journey through Acts if you don't
believe me) but it is without doubt the safest planet to live
on.

Cheapskates

I am including a little monologue called 'The man who
supplied the rope' in this section because I have recently
become very aware that some species of unauthorised fire
are quite subtle. Jesus turned the tables over in the
Temple courtyard, no doubt provoking frustration and
anger in those who had been busily short-changing visitors who needed Temple currency in order to buy animals
and birds for sacrifice. The Son of God was absolutely
furious with these cheapskates.

Here's my question. Whose tables would he be turning
over in this age? What kind of short-changing is going on
in the Christian church of the twenty-first century? When
people come to those who are supposed to know, and
offer themselves as brand new followers of Jesus, what do
they get in return? Many are well looked after and treated with love and respect, but I hear about far too many
suffering individuals who find themselves wrapped in
some crazy, uncomfortable net. This net is made up of bits
and pieces of unconsidered verses from the Bible, or
elements of cultural behaviour that have acquired a pseu-
do-spiritual status. They have very little to do with how

people actually think and feel and cope with the world, perhaps because reality is too challenging to groups that have cobbled together a way of staying safe, and are not about to have that security threatened.

You think I'm being harsh? Wait until Jesus comes into the Temple courtyard and gets going on the spiritual cheapskates of this age. I get so sick of meeting people who have been shut down as whole human beings and forced into choosing whether to give in or get out. Jesus never shoved them into that corner, but he knows who did.

Oh, by the way, did I mention that this piece is meant to be light and humorous? Oh no, I forgot. We don't want to get too heavy, do we? This chap probably sounds rather like indecisive Jim Trott from that wonderful series *The Vicar of Dibley*.

The man who supplied the rope to Jesus

I do rope. That's all I do. I make rope, cut rope, sell rope, deliver rope and go after people who owe me money for rope. I also do a second-hand stall in Bethlehem once a month called Money for Old Rope. I shall probably marry a rope by mistake in my sleep one day. I work just outside the Temple in a sort of tent that's held up by ropes, with a big sign over the top that's got a picture of some rope and great big letters made out of thin rope saying: I Make and Supply Sandals. Only joking – it doesn't. It says Rope.

Anyway, you are not going to credit what happened this morning. You really are not. This bloke, right? Walks past my tent into the Temple courtyard. Looks like someone who runs something somewhere, know what I mean.

Then, a few minutes later, out he comes again. His face! You should have seen his face. Tell you what. I've met some hard cases in my time. You do when you're in rope. But this bloke – ooh, dear!

Marches up, mouth all grim, eyes all blazing, and he says, 'Got any rope?'

Well, I'm surrounded by mountains of rope, aren't I? 'Rope World', that's me. However, I decide sarcasm might not be the most favoured option right now, so I just say, 'Er, no, no, no, no, no, yes. Lots. What variety do you require?'

'Knotted,' he says, teeth all clenched. 'Heavy knots. Easy to swing with one hand.'

So off he strides with a length of my best in his strong hands, and after a bit there's a shouting and a crashing and a bleating and a commotion like I never heard before. And feathers! Feathers drifting up into the sky, closely followed by the very cross pigeons they must have come off. It was chaos!

Out he comes again after a couple of minutes and slaps that rope down on the table in front of me.

'Nice bit of rope that,' he says, 'thanks.'

Sounds like an expert.

'You in rope yourself, then?' I ask.

'No,' he says, still grim, but with a little flicker of a smile, 'I'm a carpenter by trade, but I do a bit of house clearance on the side. Cheers, mate.'

And away he goes.

Five

Wasted weakness

Thorny questions

Here's a question for you. What is it that impedes Christians? Stock answers to this question include sin, disobedience, poor prayer life, failure to read the Bible and lack of fellowship. It will not have escaped your notice (I hope) that these are all areas of negative behaviour. We too easily forget that, in Matthew 23, Jesus reframed the Ten Commandments into a list of two wholly positive ones, both of which contain and displace negative behaviour rather than majoring and dwelling on it.

Bearing all this in mind, I would like to offer my own list of impeding factors. It includes principles, faked spiritual excitement, excessive religious behaviour, and, the one I invite you to consider for a few moments, waste of weakness. How is it possible to waste weakness? Remember this passage from 2 Corinthians 12?

> To keep me from becoming conceited because of these surpassingly great revelations, there was given me a thorn in the flesh, a messenger of Satan, to torment me. Three times I pleaded with the Lord to take it away from me. But he said to me, 'My grace is sufficient for you, for my power is made

perfect in weakness.' Therefore I will boast all the more gladly about my weaknesses, so that Christ's power may rest on me. That is why, for Christ's sake, I delight in weaknesses, in insults, in hardships, in persecutions, in difficulties. For when I am weak, then I am strong.

There you are, then. The stunning fact is that God's power is made perfect in our weaknesses. Perhaps because the words are fairly familiar, we sort of think we know what this means, don't we? But the concept is worth dwelling on. Weakness is not a barrier to service. On the contrary, if we are brave enough to wholeheartedly offer God those areas in our lives where we fail, he is likely to recycle them and use them for his own purposes, Paul's conversion and subsequent career being a perfect example of this phenomenon. Even more importantly, his strength will actually be more clearly demonstrated to the rest of the world, precisely because he works through us despite our failings.

Our weaknesses. Great opportunities. Let's not waste them. Here's a thorny question. Does all this actually mean anything? After all, it is so much *not* the way of the world. Want another one? Here you are then. Are you held back by a sense of inadequacy and weakness? What would it cost to surrender yourself to God as a public example of the miraculous work of the Holy Spirit? Maybe God is expecting too much? Why shouldn't we focus mainly on our strengths? What do you think? Here's one suggestion about what we might do:

Let's all give up – now !

You might be tempted to agree with this initiative after reading my last section. I think there are two things to be said about this starkly uncompromising proposition, certainly as far as followers of Jesus are concerned. First, it really is a very bad idea. Secondly, it is a great idea, the Holy Grail of true Christian endeavour, as opposed to religious ambition or human optimism.

First of all, why is it a bad idea?

In 1995 Bridget and I and three of our children spent one Sunday morning in a large tent in Soweto, the enormous black township that stands on the edge of Johannesburg, the capital city of South Africa. We were there with hundreds of black South Africans to join in with a Christian service of outreach and celebration. It was a year since national elections had spelled an end to the evils of apartheid, and there was an atmosphere of deep but guarded relief and hope. The singing was spectacular. In particular we were moved to tears by a song that consisted of only three words, sung again and again in those vibrantly surging harmonies that, in this part of the world, are fuelled by accumulated passion in the hearts and souls of those who participate.

'Never give up, never give up, *never* give up . . .'

The church in South Africa was and is highly influential in the process of political change, playing a crucial role in avoidance of the bloodbath that many, many people had feared. So, no, without denying the huge challenges still faced by that bruised nation, of course those suffering people don't want to give up, and nor should we. Following Jesus has never been easy, but in every way that will ever count in this world, it is the only game in town. We are for Jesus, and we must never give up.

Reverse direction with a screech of brakes. Why should we all give up – now? Simply because a lot of our carefully labelled strivings are at best harmless but a complete waste of time, and at worst a source of confusion and frustration to those who struggle so hard to make them mean something.

Let's give up waiting to become Christians who are wonderful enough to be used by God. We'll be waiting forever. God loves us exactly as we are, and far too much to leave us as we are. Let him do the changing, and we'll co-operate whenever we can, but in the meantime we need to get on with the job.

Let's give up any attempt to make the Holy Spirit happen. I have already referred to the unauthorised fire mentioned in Leviticus 10. Sometimes it looks and sounds very convincing. Words and music and lights and buildings and visual effects can be truly wonderful, and they might be gateways to the outer courtyard of the Kingdom of God, but, in themselves, they are not God. The old Christian adage remains as true as ever. Find out what God is doing and join in. It's the only safe way.

Finally, let's begin the process of giving up our precious rights, our treasured certainties, our adherence to a personal religious agenda that is more likely to close doors then open them. Let's give up anything, in fact, that impedes the work of the Holy Spirit in and through us. The list goes on, but that will do for now.

Let's decide that we will never give up on Jesus, and let's do our very best to give up anything that gets in the way. Now? That's a good idea. Yes, this would be an excellent time to start.

An Englishman's house is his crumbling castle

I feel very reluctant to take my own advice as expressed in the previous paragraph, but perhaps I should. When I started putting this book together, I made a pact with myself that I would not chicken out of speaking about my deepest, darkest insecurities. Now, as I write under the heading of 'Wasted Weakness', conscience compels me to release the mad son who has hitherto been imprisoned in the west-wing attic of my mind (too much exposure to Edgar Allen Poe as a child), and offer him up for public scrutiny. Seriously, I am *so* deeply ashamed of my lack of practical ability. No joke. I am to DIY what Mike Tyson is to ear surgery. I haven't a clue, and I have passed this comprehensive lack of skills on to my four children. We are all the kind of people who bodge a job and have to call a man in to put it right, or, much more wisely, call a man in right at the beginning and let him bodge it in a more professional manner.

There you are, you see! I've started joking about it again, as though I don't really feel that bad about the wretched things I've done to rawlplugs, and the deep holes in my walls that vomit Polyfilla out as soon as my back is turned, and end up stuffed and swamped with oceans of thick emulsion that takes an eternity to dry, but does at least temporarily hide the shameful truth. Oh, I do so *hate* it all.

I suppose it came to a head when we sold our house a while ago. The experience reminded me of a cartoon that was stuck on the wall of our poorly decorated, tile-depleted kitchen for some years while the kids were growing up. It depicted a hamster wheel. Inside the wheel were four hamsters, mother, father and two little ones. As they all paddled industriously away one of the children was saying, 'Are we there yet, daddy?'

Leaving aside the sadder, darker and more far-reaching implications of that scenario (I wish I'd never reminded myself of it now), our attempt to understand and complete the business of finally 'unloading' our house had that same air of hopelessness about it. Somewhere out there, in the rarefied atmosphere of institutions and processes that we were totally unable to understand, we assumed that we must be being moved closer to a point where, to put it bluntly, the buyers had the house, and we had the money. But it never actually seemed to happen. The wheel went round and round and round but we didn't arrive anywhere.

On some not very deep level, of course, my real fear, as one who had let his home down in a myriad ways, was that our house, never mind our lives, would not bear close examination. Guests have to be nice about the place where you live. They walk into your hall and say things like: 'What a beautiful home you have.' They don't usually add: 'But tell me, why is the skirting board parting company with the wall just down there by the dining-room door, and perhaps you could fill me on why there's a dark brown stain running down the corner of the window frame, just above the place where there's a split in the window sill? It's almost as though there's a leak that's been allowed to dribble down over a long period and damage the wood . . .'

Buyers and solicitors, on the other hand, are under no such obligation. Buyers come and peer and prod and write things in little notebooks and go outside and crane their necks so that they can stare worriedly at the roof, and stand on things to try to reach up into gutters that I honestly have been going to unblock for months.

My irrational fear was that, in the end, some ghastly, twenty-foot high parental-style, snarling solicitor would growl at me for presuming to imagine that our flawed, inadequately maintained pile of rubble could actually be exchanged for a price anywhere near the money that we were asking.

In a way, that's what happened. A set of enquiries arrived from the purchasers' solicitors. My ultra-defensive standpoint meant they were bound to appear sniffy and snotty to me, but the most practical man in the world might have decided that they were a tad over the top. The worm in me usually turns towards satire, and I suppose that might be the way that God most frequently discovers a strength in my weaknesses. I took great pleasure in writing a set of spoof replies to this list of questions. I didn't send them. I nearly did. I almost wish I had. But I will show *you*. I haven't showed them to anyone else. You will not be greatly surprised to hear that I have changed the name of the firm of solicitors, but the questions are only slightly edited, and I promise you that the spelling mistakes are exactly as they originally appeared.

Replies to questions from Umbrage, Hubris and Strop

1 *Is the Seller aware of any developments in the neighbourhood which might affect the property, including any order designation or proposals of any local or other authority or body having compulsory powers, involving any proposals for the development or charge of use of adjoining or neighbouring properties?*

Concerning developments in the neighbourhood that might affect the property, there are no such developments as far as I know or am aware. I am a little distracted at this precise moment by the constant din of cranes, mechanical diggers and earth movers in my back garden and in the fields immediately behind and around the house, but if anything springs to mind I shall certainly inform you at once.

2 *Has the Seller any information of any of the following matters which may at any time have affected the property which includes the grounds where appropriate:*

Flooding.

Structural building or drainage defects.

Subsidence.

Woodworm, rising damp, dry or other rot.

Electrical wiring failing to meet the requirements of the appropriate board.

Regarding Flooding, Structural or drainage problems, Subsidence, Woodworm, Rising damp, Dry or other rot and Electrical wiring that fails to meet the requirements of the appropriate board, I am happy to inform you that all of these things are firmly in place, and have been for some time.

3 *Please confirm that any remedies have been carried out by persons professionally qualified to carry out such works.*

All work on my house has been carried out by Gareth Ford, who lives three doors down, has CSE grade 3 in Woodwork *and* Metalwork and is as capable as any fully sighted person.

4 *Please give particulars of all approvals or refusals to approve plans of buildings and alterations to buildings under the By Laws during the period of the Sellers ownership of the property and in relation to any earlier period any particulars that the Seller can give. We note that you have supplied copy Planning Consents under reference WD/82/23275, 83/1464 and 90/2295.*

I am sure your clients would agree that these terms are bewilderingly subjective in nature. We human pilgrims aspire to discussing Planning Consents under references WD/82/23275 and 83/1464 and 90/2295 as though they have some kind of definable, objective reality, but the truth is that varying genetic influences and life experience will not allow us a common perspective in these and similar matters. Was it G.K. Chesterton who said that one man's completion certificate is another man's paper aeroplane? We must surely live in and embrace the mystery.

5 *With regard to the central heating at the property, when was it installed, is it the unencumbered property of the Seller, is there an existing contract with a fuel supplier and is it in good working order?*

Regarding the central heating, I must be honest and say that I am not sure if it is precisely in the centre. I always do my best to ensure that kindling and firelighters are laid on exactly the same spot on the sitting room floor on every occasion by lining them up with the mark on the ceiling, thus avoiding further burnt patches and unnecessary wear on other parts of the carpet, but I fully accept that the position may vary by an inch or two each time. I do not use a fuel supplier at present, but your clients should be aware that this situation may alter as we and, subsequently, they, exhaust the available stock of doors and shelves.

6 *Is the Seller aware of any defects in the drainage system?*

I am not aware of any defects in the drainage system, but I am happy to purchase these from a local B & Q or Homebase store, and fit them at my own expense.

7 *Is the Seller aware of any problems with the electrical system?*

I am not conscious of problems in the electrical system, but I will be able to finally check in the morning as soon as there is sufficient daylight to allow a proper examination.

8 *We enclose herewith a fixtures, fittings and contents questionnaire and would be grateful if you could arrange for the Sellers to complete sign and date the same and return it to us in due course.*

This is entirely acceptable, but please note that my Great Uncle Volney (see paragraphs 14 and 19) should be included in this list.

9 *Kindly confirm that any of the following items present at the property are included in the sale price and will remain at the property on completion:*
Light fittings down to and including bulb-holders.
Lamp shades, chandeliers and wall lights.
Fitted carpets.
Curtains, including pelmets.
Wall cupboards.
Shelves.
Kitchen units.

I cannot reasonably be held responsible for independently initiated excursions on the part of any inanimate object left in the house. Pelmets, as an obvious example, rather like cats, are known historically to be emotional, volatile and enterprising. Some have been known to travel as much as thirty or forty miles in search of their previous owners.

10 *Is the proposed sale by the Seller dependent upon a simultaneous purchase by them? If so, with regard to that transaction:*
What stage has it reached?
A small, independent, progressive one on the edge of Hampstead Heath.
Is the proposed purchase an existing property or is it in the course of construction?
No.

If in the course of construction, what is the estimated completion date?
Yes, of course.
Have mortgage facilities been approved, at least in principle?
Yes, but not in the south.

11 *Does the Seller have a specific date in mind for completion?*
   Yes, thank you for asking, I intend to celebrate completion by going for a drink with my wife at The Miller's Armpit.

12 *Kindly confirm that the Seller appreciates that vacant possession is to be given on completion and that no junk or unwanted moveables should be left on the property at completion.*
   You request that no junk shall be left behind. What on earth possesses you to suppose that I have a flat-bottomed Chinese seagoing vessel lodged on my property? The wrecked ship that I do have is strictly speaking a *Koysha*, and is of Singaporean origin. I shall be leaving that on and around the front drive, and on the patio, and in the conservatory, and on the lawn, and in the kitchen, and little bits and pieces in the hall.

13 *Kindly confirm that the Seller appreciates that any damage done to the property caused by the removal of any wall lights, shelves or other fixtures must be remedied prior to completion.*
   How can you ask? Of course I do not appreciate having to do all these fiddling repairs. In fact, to use a legal term, it constitutes '*A Bloody Nuisance*'.

14 *The Sellers have indicated that the property is occupied by a third person but they have given no indication of their age. If he or she is aged over 16, please confirm that they will sign the contract in the normal way.*

Regarding the other occupant of our house, I feel very strongly that yourselves and your clients are making a hillock out of a tussock over this matter. Great Uncle Volney is unlikely to live for more than another five to ten years at the most, and is virtually harmless so long as he is not fed red meat and is locked securely into the cupboard under the stairs at night. Uncle Volney does not wish to accompany my new wife and I on our move, and we feel that the wishes of a perfectly rational ninety year old man should be respected.

N.B. Creams, sanitary appliances and rubber gloves are stored in the space beneath the sink in the smallest bedroom.

15 *Would the Sellers be willing to accept a deposit of 5% of the purchase price if the Buyers financial circumstances make the same necessary?*

I am willing to accept unlimited sums of money from the buyers, regardless of their circumstances.

16 *Please confirm that the Seller has been given details of the covenants affecting the property and confirm that the Seller is not aware of any beach.*

You ask for confirmation that I have been given details of the covenants affecting the property, and that I am not aware of any 'beach'. I had no idea that insects were involved in black magic, and I am sorry to say that I am aware of several beaches in this area, at Eastbourne, Bexhill, Cooden and Birling Gap, to name but a few. I am, however, at a loss to understand how this could have any negative bearing on the purchase of my house.

17 *Please confirm that at completion the Buyers will be given all keys required to operate all the locks on doors, windows, garages, outbuildings etc to the property.*

It is surely unwise and obscurely arrogant for anyone to seriously claim that they have, in the most profound sense, discovered the key to anything of real importance in this tragic, weary world. I certainly have not, and I refuse to falsely raise the expectations of your clients by pretending that I have.

18 *The Sellers have indicated in reply to enquiry 6.1(g) of the Additional Property information form TA11, that a new boiler was installed in 2008. Please confirm that this is so with written proof. A copy of Breakdown Protection Certificate supplied does not suffice in that regad.*

I really must object to the way in which my second wife is described in the second line of this paragraph, and to the suggestion that she might be classified as Additional Property. Please inform me as to the exact nature of a 'Regad'. I believe Lionel Ritchie drove one in the eighties, but I may be mistaken.

19 *The Sellers seem to be indicating that there is some form of burglar alarm at the property. Can you please arrange for the Sellers to supply details of the suppliers name and address and indicate existing maintenance arrangements.*

Unfortunately our burglar alarm was stolen three months ago. However, recently I have been removing Uncle Volney from the cupboard under the stairs at bedtime and chaining him to a stake in the shrubbery beside the front door. This has proved to be a more than adequate deterrent to thieves (albeit a slight additional strain on our local Accident and Emergency Unit), and yet another excellent reason for our buyers to accept Uncle Volney as a fixture or fitting (see replies to questions 8 and 14).

20 *We are surprised to note that we have not received an EPC in respect of this property. An EPC is now a mandatory requirement for all properties being offered to the market.*

I am surprised, offended and deeply hurt to note that you are surprised to note that you have not received an EPC. Rest assured that as soon as I have worked out what an EPC is I shall be sending you several, of varying shapes and sizes, and they will be of the highest quality. My EPCs will not just be EPCs, they will be M & S EPCs.

21 *Please advise as to the exact date for the installation of the double glazing at the property.*

You will be pleased to hear that our recent week-long indoor baseball tournament has rendered this query obsolete.

22 *We understand that there have been problems with subsidence under the Seller's rear extension. Please confirm the position in that context and indicate the situation in regard to the carrying out of remedial works.*

I regard queries relating to subsidence under my rear extension as highly personal and embarrassing. I am willing to furnish a medical report to cover this matter, but close examination by the buyers or their agents will not be possible unless a substantial, trained nurse with speedy responses and an adequate receptacle is present at the expense of the buyers.

Six

The elephant in the room

Complicated beasts

Okay, why do we need to eject metaphorical elephants from our Christian world, and how difficult will that be? Patience, patience . . .

We who live in the Yorkshire Dales are, of course, blessed with a richly varied animal population. In the last few minutes, for instance, I have idly observed one neurotically slithering squirrel, two or three rabbits, and the unquenchably manic dog from the next house all passing across the hayfield outside my study in various directions. The abrupt rusty chuckle of a rocketing pheasant down by the main gate was probably triggered by that exuberant canine presence. Meanwhile, immediately beneath my window in our strangely regular little rectangle of a garden, the smaller birds communicate with an impressive range of twittering skills, as they engage in their usual nervous defence of life and territory.

So, lots of different creatures. Where are these elephants?

Sadly, little children of all ages, I am speaking of metaphorical elephants, the ones with the largest ears of all, as I am sure you know, and you will not find them outside. You will find them inside. You will find them in rooms, but only one at a time.

'The elephant in the room.'

Just a quick moan. We are periodically infected by these linguistic viruses, and I suppose they just have to be put up with until they run their course. Some seem ineradicable. Can we really not describe wild extremes of experience without mentioning roller-coasters? Why are conclusions that are reached after careful consideration available only 'at the end of the day'? As for that ghastly business of indicating speech marks by waggling two fingers on each hand at head height – oh, please don't get me started.

Ah, well, maybe before they go thundering off to Metaphoria or wherever they came from, the elephants can teach us something.

The 'elephant in the room', so far as I understand the expression, refers to some hugely significant consideration or issue that is visible, as it were, to all those present, but acknowledged by nobody. For us Christians this space-consuming pachyderm might sometimes actually be God. Not on formal religious occasions. Then, we are happy to dress the animal in all kinds of finery, point it out to each other with ritualistic fervour, and even address it with the carefully symmetrical respect and passion that corporate Christianity is certain it deserves.

When it comes to the ragged informality of day-to-day living, however, it is often easier and more convenient to reach an unspoken agreement that the creature has disappeared as abruptly and totally as one of those massive trucks or aircraft magicked away so mysteriously by American magicians.

It has not actually disappeared, of course, any more than David Copperfield's giant props cease to exist. This particular elephant is, most annoyingly and disruptively at times, always present. Yes, God is in the room, whether we want him there or not, asking to be involved and influential in decisions and conclusions of every conceivable size and shape. Divine bullying simply does not happen, so the eternal choice is always there, and we nervous souls must always make it. Shall we consciously allow him to be one of us, and all of us, and Lord of us? Or shall we be like those children who cover their eyes with their hands and hope that no-one can see them? In which case, God will be none of us, and not even a part of us, and there will be very little point in bothering.

Nowadays Bridget and I do our best to remain committed to the notion that God is always in the room, ready to support or wreck or alter our feeble plans in any way he wants. Will we be able to fulfil that commitment as time goes by? Who knows? Sometimes, most of the time, hardly any of the time, now and then. We are weak and vulnerable, and the will of God does not invariably appeal. Pray for us. We need it.

I should add that for some Christians the elephant in the room is the fact that there is no elephant in the room, but that's getting a bit metaphysical, and when you end up with metaphorical elephants engaged in metaphysical activities, it's definitely time to call a halt. Shovelling up the mess that those complicated beasts leave behind them is such a chore. Let's leave it at that.

Jumbo-sized pride and the job in hand

The deliberate avoidance of these creatures can often be a group activity. I was involved in one of these some years ago.

The church is continually having to drag itself out by the roots from some situation or ethos that has become more damaging than beneficial. Aspects of the evangelical church in the United Kingdom (and perhaps North America as well) during the seventies and eighties offer a vivid example of this. The Christian community was a very small pond (it is becoming little more than a shallow puddle now), and thus presented an opportunity for those who would never be more than tiddlers in the real world to behave as if they were very large fish indeed. What kind of fish? Coy, they were not. Post-embryonic rock musicians, writers of dull but worthy books, jugglers who dropped things, dancers whose removal of any remnant of sex from their performances suggested that gender itself was a sin, all pronounced and pontificated about the Christian faith as though they had been commissioned by God himself. Of course, there were notable exceptions to this dismal rule, but, generally speaking, a distinct set of behaviours and attitudes and cheap rewards inhabited and thrived in this frenzy of easy achievement.

How am I so sure about all this? Easy to answer. I was one of them. And I have to be honest. I think most of us secretly knew what was going on. How could we have pretended to avoid such regular glimpses of this massive elephant of self-delusion and pride? So delighted were we by opportunities opening up for us to show off and acquire a skinny variety of fame that we bought into all the aforementioned rubbish with a sort of greedy enthusiasm. I think I panicked about this just in time. I began to see the pitfalls that existed, and I sensed that the real rewards would come from identifying and getting involved in the things that God actually wanted me to do. After that I probably failed and succeeded in about equal measure, but at least I was aware of the problem. Perhaps there are wider implications. What do you think?

The elephant that occupies a third of the world

I have said that Bridget and I are involved with Toybox, the street child charity. This is a wonderful organisation, and it's all about children, kids of every age who have nowhere to live, no-one to care for them, and very little hope of being rescued from the devastation of prostitution, gang membership and a selection of other horrors that are likely to overwhelm them, without help from projects funded and supported by charities like Toybox.

Last year the news was full of stories about a group of men trapped hundreds of feet below ground in a Chilean mine. Massive resources were employed in devising and carrying out a rescue operation, and every single miner was brought safely to the surface. I sincerely thank God for that, but it is heartbreaking to reflect that there are hundreds of thousands of children all over Central and South America who are trapped in the darkness of poverty and homelessness. They cry out to anyone who will listen that they also desperately need rescuing from circumstances that are completely beyond their control.

Images from our trips to that part of the world fill my mind. I remember little nine year old Bettina, sitting on a cold stone seat in the darkness of Salvador City with her face buried under Bridget's arm, hoping that this sudden and unexpected oasis of safety might last forever. It didn't, of course. Who knows where Bettina is now, or what is happening to her?

Unlike those miners, children like these do not find the spotlight of world news shining upon them, and the resources available for their support and rescue are risibly small. Organisations like Toybox exist to remedy this situation through their partnerships with projects that are committed to the provision of preventative work, accommodation and moral and psychological support for children who are battling to survive in a very tough world. In this world, kids like little Bettina may not be considered important enough to get a mention in the national press, but I suspect that in heaven everything that happens to and for her is front page news.

I don't want to say much more about this, except that the needs of neglected, poverty-stricken men, women and children all over the world constitute one of the most disturbing, room-dominating elephants in the church today. Christians have an awful lot to say, sometimes with very little visible love, about issues of sin that need to be strongly addressed in the community of the church. You will hear very little about the sin of greed.

We need to be careful. This particular elephant may become so large that there is no longer space in the room.

Small but annoying elephants

These elephants do vary in size and significance, of course. As an older teenager I remember going to a Christian talk with a group of my church contemporaries. We all took ourselves a little too seriously at the time, which was unfortunate, because we wasted a whole evening listening intently to a speaker who was either genuinely brilliant and had things to say that were far beyond our capacity to understand, or was just very skilled at verbal obfuscation. None of us understood a word he said, but we didn't admit this until after we'd left. We had all been sitting in half darkness on the back row near the door, so we could have left without causing a fuss. If just one of us had had the courage to whisper the dreadful and obvious truth, the rest of us would have been off to the pub like a herd of wildebeest stampeding away from a lion.

Oh, I could have killed that elephant!

Of course, I can't remember anything at all about the talk, other than the fact that it went on for about three weeks. However, if you want to share the experience get someone to read the following passage to you, and imagine that there are another forty-nine points still to be made. See you in the pub.

It really is very simple

Good evening. The post-Kantian negation of teleological viewpoints is, of course, like the demise of ontological attitudes, inevitable; and moral autonomy as a function of quasi-rational authority is, in terms of man, a conceptual truism. Furthermore, our reference for authentification in questions of extrinsically administered codes is dependent upon pre-legislative concepts of desirable general or specific conduct. However, given the exclusion of non-relevant analogous pseudo-concepts, and bearing in mind that any rational dismissal of an argument for ultimately rational origins on the basis of fundamental irrationality is hardly rational, there may be a case for guarded acceptance of a collective strata of consciousness which, in the absence of alternative contemporary terminology we might call God. It really is very simple.

Happy Christmas!

How do you react to the idea that 'having a happy Christmas' is the elephant in the room for some folk? My mother, who was delightful in every other way, was a pain in the neck when the season of jollity came along. A little cloud of doom and gloom floated above her head, and accompanied her like a depressed barrage balloon from room to room whenever she joined our family for Christmas. I suppose it was understandable really. A difficult marriage that had resulted in eruptions at many family events, particularly this one, left her with a jaundiced view of the December festivities.

My mother was and is not alone. For many people, Christmas is one of the most testing times of all. Recently bereaved widows and widowers, for instance, can go through agonies at this time of year. Friends of ours in this position have explained that they just want to be left alone on a day when, however many people are around, they experience an aching loneliness that is almost more than they can bear. Sometimes it is easier to sit in a corner and simply wait for it all to end.

Some who have always enjoyed warm conviviality at Christmas (good for them!) find all this very difficult to understand. A fully functional family is a marvellous blessing, but for those who have battled through the tangled undergrowth of emotional or physical trauma in childhood, it can be a teeth-gritting reminder of bad, bad things.

My wife and I miss my mother terribly. We would love her to be around, even with her barrage balloon attached. But as I remember the roots of her pain, and I think about friends who dread Christmas or New Year or any other festival because they are blighted by shadows of the past, my heart goes out to them. The world they live in at these times is a dark and lonely one. There is no war between their worlds and ours, just the need for a friendly wave, sensitive invitations and the occasional visit.

And now, just to cheer you up, here's somebody who really is sick to the back teeth with *everybody* in her family.

Christmas is great!

Christmas is great, Christmas is good,
We'll have a good stir of the old Christmas pud.
When family arrive I will struggle and strive,
To smile and wish them good cheer,
But when they depart there'll be joy in my heart,
And I'll laugh as they all disappear.

Great Uncle Roy is a cheerful old boy,
But as soon as he's finished his meal,
He flops in a chair and he poisons the air,
Like a flatulent elephant seal.
Roy's cousin Zeke refuses to speak,
To his dead brother's half-sister May,
He's still seeing red about something she said,
On the morning of Armistice Day.

The kids come and feast like a plague from the east,
And their manners are less than appealing,
My granddaughter Rose sticks her peas up her nose,
And there's ketchup all over the ceiling.
Jimmy's a veggie and so's his twin Reggie,
Their diet is marmite and rice,
If they deviate from it they're likely to vomit,
In stereo – not very nice.

Phyllis and Joan are certain to moan,
'The potatoes are tasteless and knobbly,
The custard's too runny, the pudding tastes funny,
That jelly's suggestively wobbly.
These crackers were dear in the pound shop last year,
They don't crack, they go phut, it's pathetic,
The paper hats tear when exposed to the air,
And the jokes are a mild anaesthetic.'

Philip and Jane are angry with Wayne,
Who feels disapproved of by Paul,
Paul hates his mother, and Colin her brother,
And Colin despises them all.
When I'm ready to scream they run out of steam,
And they doze while I clean up the grot,
My half-eaten turkey is bright-eyed and perky
Compared with this comatose lot.

Christmas is great, Christmas is good,
We'll have a good stir of the old Christmas pud.
When family appear I'll be full of good cheer,
I'll smile and I'll wish them all well,
But when they depart there'll be joy in my heart,

And I'll wish they would all go to Helen's next year,
after all her house is just as big as mine,
and I don't really see why she shouldn't take a turn,
After all, she is my sister, and it seems only fair that. . .

Seven

Bringing the Bible alive

Proper use

Do you find it strange and frustrating that those who claim to believe in the power and significance of the Bible so often seem to go out of their way to present it in as boring and inaccessible a manner as possible? I do – find it strange, I mean. There is a maddening perversity about the way in which major components of spiritual freedom are carefully employed in the building of blank and impenetrable walls, barriers that effectively keep the world out and the church in. What a tragedy that, in the minds of many, the Bible has become a black, boring brick of a thing that helps to separate God from the 'real' world.

Play with it, I say. Read it for pleasure. Take it to pieces. Question it. Study it intelligently. Turn it upside down and look at it through a bit of broken glass. Give it a blue cover. Give it a rainbow cover. Take the cover off. Above all, react to it honestly. If you regard some words of Jesus as inexplicable or unfair or difficult to square with the rest of his teaching, give your view an airing. God is grown-up enough to handle it, even if many Christians aren't.

It really is difficult for many of us to unstick ourselves from the notion that ponderous pseudo-reverence has real value in the kingdom of God. It doesn't. It's ridiculous. The way of Jesus was and is to be among ordinary people in the place where they live, not in some rarefied, oppressively rigid ethos where nothing actually happens, but a lot of solemn nodding goes on. Allowing the Bible to come to life is a hugely important part of avoiding such nonsense. Be respectful to God but please don't make a fool of him.

Here are some things you can try.

Have a look at verses 5 to 8 in Matthew 6. Jesus is talking about prayer. Get someone to read it in a boringly monotonous tone, and then ask someone else to read it like a mother talking to a small, much-loved child. You could also try reading the parable of the Prodigal Son like a fairy tale instead of a teaching aid. Enjoy yourselves. Enjoy the Bible.

If you are in a group, give everyone a piece of paper and ask them to Google their own minds on the subject of 'Bible'. In other words, write down every little scrap, however ragged, of memory, experience, attitude, disappointment, revelation, rumour and anything else that comes to mind. Tell each other some of the things you wrote. Be careful, though. You might end up being fascinated by Scripture.

Living love?

I once bewildered and annoyed my god-son by giving him a Christmas present that appeared to be nothing more than a handful of those large chocolate coins that are wrapped tightly in shiny golden paper. Muttering insincere thanks, he handed one of the coins to his sister, unwrapped another and started to nibble on it. Suddenly there was a cry of surprise from his sister. Inside her chocolate coin wrapper she had discovered a tightly folded twenty-pound note, the Christmas present actually intended for her brother. Leaving aside the difficulty of separating one small girl from what she considered to be *her* twenty-pound note and giving it to its rightful owner, it was quite a good idea. Well, I thought so anyway.

Some Bible verses are like that. Easily dismissed and well worth unwrapping. I have my own little list of these productive collections of words, and one of my very favourite verses in the Old Testament is Job 29:24: 'When I smiled at them they could scarcely believe it.'

That's what it says, and it's spoken by poor, boil-infested Job as he recalls the good old pre-boil days when he was one of the best personal representatives that God could ever have hoped for. As far as we can tell, people seemed to love the things that he said and did.

By contrast, a lot of folk get very fed up with Christians nowadays. A lot of it is our own fault, of course. We do seem to have made an art out of patronising gittishness, especially on television for some strange reason. I hide miserably behind the sofa, like a cat with gastric problems, when someone on one of those audience participation programmes fixes a coyly sparkling smile on their face and begins their first sentence with the words, 'As a follower of the Lord Jesus Christ, I would have to say that . . .'

I suppose the smile is intended to express joy, peace and love, but it actually fills me, a born again Christian (is there some other sort?), with a confusing turmoil of anger, shame and frustration. I have never actually thrown up or down behind that settee of mine (carpets cost money after all), but I have come close.

What a shame these enamel smiles are, because one of the most captivating things about being a staggering, faltering follower of Jesus like me is the realisation that it involves offering a genuine smile to people in situations where they least expect it. The smile is not just a facial expression, of course, although a real one can be amazingly effective. It could be a garden sorted out for a beleaguered friend. It could be the provision of a well supplying clean water for a small community in the slums of Bangladesh. It could be an hour spent with a lonely, elderly person. It might be an anonymous gift or unexpected forgiveness or a temporary abandonment of the rules, or telling a benevolent lie to your brother about you not really wanting the last sausage so he might as well have it.

All these things and many more besides are regular features in the lives of Christians who are more interested in being Jesus in the world than merely talking about him. And yes, of course it is true that many, many non-Christians are continually involved in acts of love as well. Is there a difference? I suppose it might be that Job, the generous chap who speaks the words quoted in this verse, and all those others who have embarked on the difficult, fascinating, confusing, hope-filled path of Christian living, believe that we have discovered the well-spring of love, however and wherever it is expressed.

Jesus sets a good example. April Fool's Day didn't exist when he was here in the flesh, but folk must have wondered sometimes. He said stupid things that could only be sick jokes or hopelessly inflated expectations.

Examples? What about saying a dead girl wasn't dead, but sleeping? Such a bad joke. Such an irresponsible statement to heartbroken parents. Stupid, eh?

Remember the widow of Nain? Devastated by her son's death. His heart went out to her. Fine, but look what he actually said.

'Don't cry.'

Don't cry? Appalling counselling technique. Absolute rubbish. Not funny, and not helpful.

What about his preposterous claim to have 'overcome death'? Honestly! How disappointing when it ended in disaster. Crucifixion. Dead. Gone.

Of course, all this would be true, except that Jairus' daughter *did* wake up, the widow's son *was* restored to life, and Jesus *did* rise from the dead, rescuing us in the process.

It's about the Holy Spirit, isn't it? It's about believing in a power that can make silly things mean something, a power that transforms foolish-sounding promises into gloriously unexpected reality. Bucketloads of divine generosity are available for needy people. Words are needed occasionally, and smiles that come from the heart are wonderful, but bona fide love offers a meal, not a recipe. The Bible preaches love, but let's ask God for enough courage and faith to get personally and practically involved in the process of distribution. Amaze people, as Job did, with the smile of God.

Sitcom Scripture

I don't know if this next bit would make God smile, but I do know that it is going to seriously date me. Quite a lot of people do remember Frank Spencer, that extraordinary character created by Michael Crawford in the hugely successful comedy series *Some mothers do have 'em*, but to younger folk the name means little. Frank was an effete, blunderingly inadequate individual, devoted to his wife Betty and his baby daughter Jessica, but continually failing in every department of his life. His singular vocal delivery has been imitated to death by impressionists. Why have I resurrected it for the purposes of this sketch? All right, if I'm honest, because it's one of the voices I can actually 'do', and secondly because the idea of Spencer combined with Zechariah is so wonderfully bizarre.

Frank Spencer interviewed as Zechariah, father of John the Baptist

I : What happened, Zechariah?
Z : Well, I was in the emple mindin' my own sacramental business. And a angel come in.
I : You mean he came in through the door?
Z : No – he manifested hisself.
I : Oh.
Z : And he got mad at me.
I : Why did he get mad at you?
Z : Well, he told me I was going to have a child. And I said, 'I can't.' And he said, 'Why not?' And I said, 'Because I'm a man.' And I didn't like the way he looked at me when I said that. In fact I took deep expectation to his manner. And then he said, 'No, your wife Elizabeth's going to have a child, and the child's name's goin' to begin with J.'
I : How did you feel about that?
Z : I was quite pleased. I thought, Nice – we'll call her Jessica.
I : Jessica the Baptist . . .
Z : But he said, 'No, it's going to be a boy called John.' And that's when he got even madder with me, 'cause I was gobsmacked.
I : What did he do?
Z : He smacked me in the gob. He said I wouldn't be able to talk for nine *months*! I was dumb! I was dumb! I was completely dumb! Can you imagine me dumb?

I : Err, no – so what did you do?

Z : I decided to go home and share with my wife Elizabeth all that I had come to pass.

I : But you couldn't talk.

Z : No, but in my house I had some piles of pieces of papyrus. I had many, many piles of pieces of papyrus, many, many piles, and I picked a piece of papyrus from one of my piles.

I : Aaah...

Z : And I scribed some words on it.

I : What were the words that you – er – scribed?

Z : 'I got a bit o' trouble, Betty . . .'

Situation tragedy

Eastenders is certainly not a situation comedy. On the contrary, it seems to be an unremittingly grim situation tragedy. Most of us wouldn't last more than a couple of days in the storm of conflict and emotion that rages through the gelatinous gloom of Albert Square each week. Why have I chosen Phil Mitchell for the following sketch? Well, there's something unmistakably Old Testament about him, don't you think?

Phil Mitchell of *Eastenders* as Philip, the disciple who met the eunuch

I : What exactly happened to you, Phil?

P : Well, I was in the pub –

I : *The Queen Vic*, you mean?

P : Never 'eard of it, no I was in *The Dave* –

I : *The Dave*?

P : Yeah, *The King Dave* – an' this angel come up an' told me to go down the desert road round Gazza way, so –

I : Gazza? You mean Gaza.

P : Whatever. Anyway, along come this Ainsley 'arriot, an' –

I : Ainsley Harriot came along?

P : Naaaah, Aramaic rhyming slang, innit? Ainsley 'arriot – chariot.

I : Aaah, right . . .

P : An' inside the Ainsley 'arriot there was this Eefyopeyan.

I : Eefyopeyan?

P : You takin' the arc?

I : The arc?

P : Yeah, the archangel.

I : Taking the arch – aah, the Michael!

P : Yeah, you takin' the arc?

I : No-no-no! So you met this Eefyopeyan – I mean Ethiopian?

P : Yeah, Eefyopeyan. 'E was one o' them er – 'e was a yoonuck.

I : A yoonuck?

P : Yeah, 'e 'ad no – 'e 'ad no – 'ad no er – 'e 'adn't got no er – 'e 'adn't got no-one to 'elp 'im read Isaiah. So I 'elped 'im out like.

I : And then?

P : Well, I baptised 'im in the river, din' I?

I : So now he'll go to heaven.

P : Well, actually, 'e's already in 'eaven.

I : What do you mean?

P : My bruvver Grant come along just as the Eefyopeyan
went under the water, an' – well, Grant's a few verses
short of a chapter, ain't 'e? 'E jumped in an' 'eld the
bloke's 'ead under the water for ten minutes.
I : Oh, dear.
P : Yeah, you can't tell Grant. Know what I mean? An' then
I suddenly found meself back in *The King Dave*.
I : You must have been transported by the Spirit.
P : Naah, I was stone cold sober. I'd only 'ad a small beer.
I : Thanks er – thanks, Phil.

The possibilities in this area are endless, of course. If we
were looking for someone to play doubting Thomas, for
instance, what better choice could there be than Victor
Meldrew, the famous hero of *One Foot In the Grave*?
   'I do not *believe* it!'

The strange message of Hebrews

There are some bits of the Bible that we may not want to
bring alive, and this could be one of them. Hebrews
13:11–14: have you ever noticed this passage? I hadn't until
my wife pointed it out to me. This is how it reads.

The high priest carries the blood of animals into the most
Holy Place as a sin offering, but the bodies are burned outside the camp. And so Jesus also suffered outside the city
gate to make the people holy through his own blood. Let us,
then, go to him outside the camp, bearing the disgrace he
bore. For here we do not have an enduring city, but we are
looking for the city that is to come.

In an alternative translation, the final phrase in the penultimate sentence of this passage is translated 'to share in his disgrace'. What can this phrase possibly mean? I am still on a journey of understanding towards the secret of this aspect of following Jesus, but I think it will repay concentration, prayer and a jolly good, hard think. In or out of the city? Pride or disgrace? Give it some meditational wellie.

In the meantime, I can at least offer you this short poem, which I read to myself from time to time, especially when my head inflates like a ballon and floats up to a dangerous distance from my feet.

To share in his disgrace

> Father, grant our heartfelt prayer,
> That we may turn aside,
> From wearisome entanglement
> In pettiness and pride
> Let these tarnished souls of ours,
> Reflect the Saviour's face,
> And may we never be ashamed
> To share in his disgrace.

Authentic identity

Let's bring one more bit of Bible to life. In Mark 5, we meet a character who benefited enormously from his encounter with Jesus. He was able to rediscover his original and authentic identity through healing. What he would think of my version, I can't begin to imagine.

Pig man

Good morning, ladies and gentlemen. Yes, I am the famous Pig Man, and I am a Gerasene and an ex-nutter. I don't mind admitting I used to be a nutter. Actually, I didn't know I was a nutter, but I was. I *was* nutty.

'How nutty were you?' I hear you ask, in curious but caring tones.

Well, I was as nutty as a nut-flavoured container fashioned entirely out of crushed nuts and filled to the absolute brim with huge numbers of the nuttiest nuts in the entire history of particularly nutty nuts. I was (*pause*) a little unstable. I lived in the graveyard among the tombs (I must have been nuts!) and I had these three hobbies (*counts off on his fingers*). I'd do a spot of crying out in the morning – that would usually get a bit of a crowd together, a couple of hours of cutting myself with stones in the afternoon – crowd thinned out a bit when I did that (well, I was naked and a bit wild-eyed, to be fair), and then I'd probably spend the evening, you know, not letting myself be chained up.

I'd go, (*feebly*) 'No-o-o, you're not chaining me up!'

I was quite fierce really, though I say it myself.

And then, at bedtime I'd just lay myself out on a slab, a gravestone, and – you know – rest in peace. And in case you're wondering, I was (*pause*) dead comfortable, thank you.

Anyway, this bloke turned up and called all these demons out of me. I mean, I never knew it was demons causing trouble. I thought it was a nut allergy. Too many brazils or too much coffee and walnut cake or something. Two thousand demons living inside *me*! They never paid any rent or council tax.

So, after that, all these demons started talking to this bloke out of *my mouth* and he talked back to them. Oh, don't mind me, I thought, you lot just carry on. Be my guests – well, two thousand of them already were. Not for long, though, because the bloke told 'em they could move out of *(pats his chest)* this des res into a load of pigs on the hillside. I mean, I never saw 'em go, but I suppose they must have done, because all those porkers shot off grunting and barking down the hill and drowned themselves in the lake. Two thousand pigs in a big pile at the bottom of the lake, with a little cross demon inside each one – you don't see that every day, do you?

I asked that bloke who he was. Said he was the Son of God. And they called *me* nutty! I like him, though. I wanted to go with him when he got in his boat to go back wherever he came from, but he wouldn't let me. Sent me off to tell all the locals what had happened. So I did. Had no fight left in me. Anyone could have chained me up. Most of the   people I told were amazed. One minute I was naked and two thongs short of a sandal, next minute I'm middle-class and boring. Some didn't believe my story about the pigs. Can't blame 'em, can you? My Uncle Josh was the worst, he always is. Do you know what he said?

'What a load of gammon – and what a waste of bacon! You're a nutter, you are . . .'

Eight

Sacred cows

What is a sacred cow?

What is a sacred cow? I suppose it's a relatively worthless (sorry cows) object or way of behaving or idea that has been afforded a significance or value that is way beyond it's actual worth. The church is full of them. Funny voices, things you do with your arms, things you do with your legs, things you don't do with your arms and your legs, things you do with your face, buildings, myriad styles and designs of ceremonial bling, collections of words, simplistic songs that have to be sung thirty-nine times for some reason – finish the list for yourself. We've only got room for a few here, but there are always casualties in wars. Let's shoot a few.

A happy medium?

What about communion? Sacred cow? Well, it can be. Just about anything can be if the heart of its intention is ripped out and replaced with some mechanical contrivance that will never be more than a poor substitute for the original. On the whole, I love the way we Anglicans do communion, the little journey from your seat, the delicate sideways jostling for position, the indecision about whether to meet the minister's eyes or not, the tiny fragments of bread and wine that make you want more of them and of the amazing things that they symbolise, the hand laid on children's heads while they are blessed or prayed for, the infinitesimal uncertainty about the appropriate length of pause before you turn and go back to your seat. I love it all, but even this event can become hollow and pointless when habit takes over from heart.

There are times, as I watch communicants returning from the rail in neat lines with solemnly bowed heads and hands clasped in front of them like footballers facing a free kick near the goal, when I wonder if we have formalised the process a little too much and removed the humanity from a sacrament that should be an exchange of warm gratitude and generous love. Judging from Paul's comments in 1 Corinthians 11, the people he addresses had gone right over the top, grabbing food greedily before anyone else could get any, and actually becoming drunk on the wine. Surely, however, there might be a happy medium? Perhaps there is a need to experiment with new kinds of communion liturgy, orders of service that include not just the informality of exchanging the peace, which some love and many loathe, but also space for heartfelt interaction with each other and with God. How will that manifest itself? I'm not sure, but I'm working on it. Let me know if you have any ideas.

In the meantime, there are of course other ways in which communion is formally and informally celebrated, and I think I have participated in just about all of them. Forgive my flippancy, but I have been wondering what would have happened if Jesus had instituted the sacrament in ways that diverge from the basic Anglican model. For instance, like this little known extract from a lost gospel.

Put the kettle on

Likewise, after supper, he took the flat wooden tray with a handle on top and sixteen round holes each containing a miniature drinking glass half filled with cherryade, and he said, 'This is my blood, shed for you, take it and – no, hold on a moment, wait till everyone's got one – Barnabas, you've got two, put one back, there's no alcohol in it, you know. Andrew, which part of "Wait" did you not understand? Peter, no, mate, take yours when you've finished passing the others round and – no, you're not going to lose out. What? Well, because you can't carry a tray in each hand and your own glass at the same time, can you? Nobody can. No, I can't. Just because I'm the Son of God. I don't do conjuring tricks, you know. Just drop them both for a moment and – no, don't actually drop them! Oh, dear! That was a metaphor, drop them! Put them down. Don't actually drop them. It was a *metaphor*. We're going to have to start all over again now, aren't we? Right, this is my Shloer, shed for you – no . . . Oh, blimey, I think this had better be the penultimate supper. Sort of dress rehearsal. We'll have another shot tomorrow. Try it with cups instead of a tray. Put the kettle on before we start. We'll call this one the Last Cuppa . . .'

Not letting God off the hook

Can the avoidance of imagination be a sacred cow? Unbelievably, it can. I have sometimes been challenged about the place of fiction in Christian writing. How can something that is not true have spiritual value for Christians?

Are we mad to ask? Am I even more mad to bother with an answer? Probably, but I will. The most vivid teaching in the New Testament was delivered in the form of fictional tales, or parables, as they are more commonly known. I am well aware that the one who created and honed these masterpieces of communication was only the Son of God, but it might just be worth considering the idea of following his example. Presentation of spiritual truth doesn't have to be dull, whatever the majority of modern preaching might suggest. Jesus used such subjects as robbery, torture, murder, failed family relationships, loss, abandonment and tearful alienation in his stories. I doubt if he was ever boring. But what was he trying to do? What were parables meant to achieve?

Apart from anything else, they were designed to entertain those audiences that are so far distant from us in time and space. I am reliably informed by Jewish theologians that Jesus would have had them rolling in the aisles with some of his neat little turns and twists. There's no point in being worthy if you can't hold the attention of your readers – is there?

Secondly, like all good fiction, secular or spiritual, these tales offered an opportunity for listeners to draw their own conclusions in their own time in a secure situation. Indeed, we might define a parable as a story that knocks on the front door while the truth slips in through a side window. And the important thing about an image like this is that, broadly speaking, you feel quite safe standing on your own doorstep. Constructive storytelling and drama allow us freedom and a protected space in which to discover new and useful ways of thinking.

Why do Christians sometimes object to fictional narrative? I suspect because it frightens them. I received a letter from a lady in America describing a passage in one of my novels as 'Lust-provoking trash.' I was slightly flattered by this comment. I had never thought myself capable of such an achievement. However, I was more puzzled than anything else. The scene in question involved a recently bereaved Christian man who is sexually tempted by an attractive woman who enters his bedroom late at night. Somehow, wonderful as the prospect appears, he manages to resist the temptation, mainly because he really does wish to be obedient to his heavenly Father. I suspect that my American critic simply could not bear the thought that in 'real life' there are struggles and pitfalls and imminent dangers for all those who seriously wish to follow Jesus.

Read good books, Christian or otherwise. Learn about relationships, and love and devastation and ecstasy, and all the other things that feed in to your understanding of what it means to be an authentic human being. The truth, as someone much wiser than me once said (and I never tire of repeating, as you may have noticed) will set you free.

After our trip to Zambia in 2004, I wrote a fictional monologue that is spoken by the father of the Prodigal Son to the assembled members of his household. It is also intended to be God the Father addressing his church. It was inspired by a conversation with a girl called Chilufya, who we met when she visited a World Vision office. She was there to ask if they might have a job available that would allow her to give up the sex-work with which she had been forced to support herself and her brother. When I asked Chilufya if she was a Christian, she said that she had grown up in the church but no longer attended.

'Will you go back to church now?' I asked.

Her eyes filled with tears.

'No,' she replied, 'God will not want me there, knowing what I have done and what I have become.'

It broke our hearts to hear this. Who turned the gospel upside down in this girl's mind? The speech by the Prodigal's father was written in direct response to this conversation, and I suppose it is exactly the kind of thing that some people find so difficult. I am putting words into the mouth of a character in one of Jesus' stories, adding to Scripture, if you like. Creating a fiction around a truth. I am entirely unrepentant. Not for one moment am I suggesting that I know what the Prodigal's father would have said, nor do I claim any wacky prophetic insight into the famous parable. Nevertheless, this fictional account may have the effect of opening minds and hearts to the central truth of God's purposes for his followers in this world, and might possibly even encourage them to go back to the Bible and find out exactly what it does say. You read it and decide for yourself.

By the way, unlike just about everything else in this book, the father's speech has been published before in *The Son of God is Dancing*[2] a book that Bridget and I wrote after our trip to Zambia. I suspect that it needs more airing. And thereby hangs a tale . . .

I debated inwardly whether to talk about this, but it would help me to sort my own thinking out, so please bear with me.

I first read this piece in public at a World Vision evening in Tonbridge. It seemed to go down well, but after the presentation a lady approached me.

'That thing you read about the Prodigal's father,' she said, 'it was all very well, but you let God off the hook. If he'd really cared about that girl you met, he would have looked after her and made sure she was okay and didn't have to work as a prostitute. Why should she end up feeling guilty and lost? It wasn't her fault. I don't think you should read things like that.'

Rightly or wrongly, I was deeply upset by those comments. Historically there has been a part of me that defaults to anger and bewilderment when I focus on the apparent neglect suffered by those who have trusted God and ended up disappointed and hurt. Spiralling down into a familiar bog of confusion, I didn't read the monologue again for a very long time. I suppose it must be a measure of my changed understanding of God that I read it quite often nowadays. I think this is because I have begun to have a new sense of the incredibly energetic and complex work that the Holy Spirit puts into our lives. I believe that there are battles we would not credit going on behind the scenes on our behalf and, dare I say it, I think that the Father heart of God is filled with pain whenever we doubt the purity and strength of his intentions. Why is it all so difficult? Pass. Why can't God do what he wants, if he's omniscient and omnipotent? Pass. Do I trust him anyway? Yes, in the high percentages mostly, and occasionally not a lot.

God doesn't want to be let off the hook either, and I for one intend to go on asking awkward questions and ranting at the Creator when my feelings are moving in that direction. But it is also true that I want to be with him in it, whatever 'it' is revealed to be. I certainly don't want to hurt him.

So, here is the father of the Prodigal pleading with his household for a little understanding.

The Prodigal's father

Thank you all for being here.

You cannot fail to be aware that my younger son has been absent from my home for many months. He asked me to give him his share of the inheritance that would one day be his due. It was his desire to leave and seek a new life elsewhere. It was, as I am sure you will understand, neither my wish nor my will that he should do this. The pain of parting from him was almost more than I could bear.

I have a letter, brought to me by a member of my household this morning. It contains details of the life my son is living now. Dark, terrible things fill his hours in the far country to which he has travelled. The person who brought this letter spoke with bitterness and derision of my boy, presumably believing that I would welcome and indeed echo his condemning tone.

My older son mocks the very notion of his younger brother being of any value to me now. His words are harsh and unyielding, filled with hate. He seems to think he pleases me when he is so cruelly dismissive. Perhaps he believes that the scorn and fury in my own heart are too profound for words.

Other, gentler souls counsel me to forget I ever had a younger son. Let it be as though he never existed. Let it be as though he were dead. Then you will find peace.

They are wrong. Only one thing will bring me peace. Only one thing will heal my broken heart. That will be the homecoming of my beloved younger son. I wept when he departed. I begged him, for his own sake, to stay. I know all too well that the life he lives in that place is a denial of all the right and good things he learned at my knee. But now hear these words. I love him. I love that boy without any condition at all. I long for him. I hold him in my heart during every hour of every day. If you truly believe that this is not so, then you certainly do not know me. My love for him will never die.

But I cannot force him to return home. He is where he wishes to be, and I must be here. I am what I am and he is what he is. I will live forever with the pain of loving him from a distance, if that is what the future holds. But let me tell you this. At the very instant when that dear lad decides to leave his life of darkness and come back where he belongs, I shall run to meet him, and I shall enfold him in my arms, and I shall shower him with presents, and I shall throw a party the like of which has never been seen in this household before. I think he will be very surprised.

And you, all of you, do not dare to speak slightingly of the son that I adore. Do not disrespect the hope of my heart. Members of my household, please be with me in this. If you love me, then love him. If you wish the best for me, then wish the very best for him.

And, my friends, if by some chance you should happen to encounter him on your travels, would you please let him know that there is a father who watches for him every day, and offers nothing but love and forgiveness if he should decide to come home. I thank you all so much for listening to me.

Positively negative

Picking up the point I made just now about not wanting to let God off the hook, I meant all that I said, but I do hope that, in the best and most constructive sense, I will never stop doing exactly that. I am sometimes accused of being negative, and I expect this is true to an extent, but these remarks are often provoked by my habit of asking questions when I don't understand things. It might be a passage of Scripture or a comment in a meeting, or a set of experiences in somebody's life that doesn't seem to make any sense at all in the context of what we read in the Bible about the caring nature of God. At one time there probably was an element of deliberate awkwardness in my dogged determination to get to the bottom of things, but nowadays I really care. I hunger for the truth, and I am especially wary of human optimism disguised as Holy Ghost inspiration. I want to meet God. I don't want to make him happen. Least of all do I want to let him off this blinking hook that we keep on mentioning. I suspect that he would be very cross if I did that. No, my glass may be only three-quarters full, but I am very keen indeed to fill it up with the genuine stuff.

It is a difficult balance, though, isn't it? As I wrote somewhere a long time ago, there's not much future in a praise album entitled *Life Stinks And Then You Die*. Sales would be minimal, and probably limited to those who actually enjoy sinking into despair. Those of us who have paddled in the shallows of the mighty ocean of God's love are anxious to share our experiences, but there is no point at all in talking as though we have taken a bathy-scape 36,000 feet down to explore the bottom of the Marianas trench, if all we've actually done is to get our feet wet.

Read in the gospels about the last three years of Jesus' life. It was not an easy walk. Ours will not be either. Lots of light, lots of darkness. Sometimes God is a presence in the midst of darkness, but the darkness doesn't always go away, and it is unhelpful to claim that it does. Be excited. Be hopeful. But do tell the truth as well. Ask and answer the important questions as truthfully as you can. What are the positive things that you can truthfully say about your encounters with God? What are the things that you hope or yearn to experience with God? Where is safety and where is danger in relation to darkness and light? By the way, I have no specific answer to this final question, but I'm sure it is worth asking.

Telling lies to universities?

I might get into trouble over this. I would like to suggest that factual truth is a bit of a sacred cow. As we all know, there are moments when truth and kindness collide, and at such times it is sometimes better for those two strong forces to shake hands and make a plan, rather than put their heads bullishly down and go blindly into battle with each other.

This view upset a friend of mine last year. I told him that I am occasionally invited to speak at university Christian Unions around the country, and I further explained that these organisations usually send me a doctrinal statement to sign and return before my visit. This statement invariably includes an assertion that the Bible is infallible and inerrant.

'I hardly bother reading it,' I added, 'I just sign the paper and send it off.'

My friend frowned as his Intensive Guilt Training kicked in.

'Do you mean that you sign something you don't believe?'

'Well, sort of, I suppose.'

'So, actually, you're lying. I don't like the sound of that.'

I writhed and wriggled a bit.

'Well, it's not exactly like that . . .'

He wasn't very impressed, but that really is the problem with so many major issues arising from serious consideration of the Christian faith. They are not *exactly* like anything – thank God. And this business of infallibility and inerrancy is a good example. I am quite sure that the Bible has been given to us in its entirety by God, so that we can be taught and entertained and informed and disciplined and inspired, but I absolutely refuse to shut down my mind when I turn its pages, and I will never become a slave to ridiculously simplistic notions that create problems where there are supposed to be solutions. I love talking to students about Jesus, and I am not going to let differences in definition get in my way, especially when it's just a question of a few squiggles on a piece of paper. You might find 1 Corinthians 9:15–27 interesting in this respect.

The truth is part of who we are as followers of Jesus, but so is the freedom to think and feel and compare and analyse and explore strange and slightly scary side-roads. I wonder if you agree? Have I got it wrong? Is everything more clear-cut and black and white than I seem to think? It's useful to think and talk honestly about our experiences of the Bible. How does it work? What is it for? And then we might ask ourselves – just how fluid is the concept of truth? Here's another good question. Did Jesus say anything that was not true? Have a look at John 7:1–10, and Matthew 11:11. You may be surprised.

Promises, promises

We Christians are able to completely trust each other, aren't we? Are we? I'm not so sure. In fact, the very suggestion seems to be accompanied by a sonorous mooing sound.

The truth is that trust can be a very heavy burden to inflict or carry, and it is yet another example of the pulpy terms that we Christians use so confidently and wrestle with so constantly. Jesus appears to have had no doubts on the subject. There is a passage in John 2 where, having deeply impressed the crowd with miraculous signs, he is clearly not about to cash in on his success by feeding on their admiration, or by satisfying their appetite for a lot more spiritual 'magic'.

> Now while he was in Jerusalem at the Passover Feast, many people saw the miraculous signs he was doing and believed in his name. But Jesus would not entrust himself to them, for he knew all men. He did not need man's testimony about man, for he knew what was in a man.

Useless at marketing, the Son of God, was he not? Wrong era, I suppose. Max Clifford could have made a fortune out of him. No, Jesus knew that, when it comes to trust, there are serious limitations in our hearts. He knew this partly through experience of other people (I don't suppose collecting payment for carpentry jobs was any easier then than it is now), and partly because, being tempted in every way exactly as we are, he could see the possibilities of betrayal and moral failure within himself.

This issue has to be raised and addressed regularly in the context of all community living. For Bridget and I, living in a formal community situation for the first time, it has become increasingly clear that dependence on each other is a crucial aspect of the work we do. But to what extent can we confidently entrust ourselves to each other? What can we wholeheartedly promise to each other and to God? I'll come back to that in a moment.

The question of trust in family life is rather different, at least in my experience. When our four children were little, they seemed to trust us completely and, by and large, we kept the promises that were implicit and explicit in our parenting. As they grew older, however, I found their inevitable discovery of my many flaws a difficult, painful thing to handle. They knew I loved them, but they had also learned that I was capable of letting them down. The positive aspect of all this was and is, of course, that we now relate more or less authentically to each other. The truth really does set you free, even if freedom is uncomfortable at times.

Having said all this, my daughter, who is now twenty-four, retains a touching and occasionally alarming trust in my ability to solve the problems that life flings randomly in her direction. Recently she locked herself out of her London flat after putting the rubbish out, wearing nothing but a dressing-gown. Being a modern girl, Kate would have felt as naked without her mobile phone as she would have done without her dressing-gown. Fortunately it was in her pocket. I was about a hundred miles away when she called to ask what she should do. Between us we got a locksmith there. It took him thirty seconds to slide a card down the crack between the door and the doorpost, push the door open, and present her with a bill for £75.

I know I can't help every time, but I would hate it if she stopped calling me when the crises come . . .

So what about the general issue of trust in our Christian lives? What kind of promises can we realistically make to

God and to each other? As I have said elsewhere, here in
our own community we have abandoned the idea that
members should make impossible vows in public. Instead,
we promise to do our best, which is actually more challenging if we take it seriously.

Personally, I have discovered a profound liberation in
releasing myself from human ambition disguised as spiritual responsibility. God keeps his promises. My record is
very patchy. I wrote the following poem (or prayer) in an
attempt to encapsulate a realisation that is both humbling
and refreshing.

I promise

Strange God, Lord, Jesus, Saviour, friend
What can I promise you?
Only one thing with no shadow of a doubt
I promise I will let you down
I feel quite sure that there will be some courtyard
    somewhere
Where a fire burns and crowds are gathered
And the test will come
And I shall feel my stomach lurch with fear
I know what I am liable to do
I'll blow my stack and throw you to the wolves
Let them tear your name to shreds
Probably retreat and come to with a shock
To find myself on some sad corner of the street
Lingering and lost beneath a lamp-post in the rain
And then I'll weep, I know I will
And wish that I could die
And never see your disappointed face again
And then, of course, my strange, close, persistent friend

You'll keep *your* promise, won't you?
To love me, love me, love me, love me
How could you do otherwise?
It is the way that you are made
I fear I have not yet received sufficient grace to smile
When I am punished with such unrestrained compassion
All in all I do not have the wisdom nor the power, sometimes
   not the will
To make wild promises about the things that I shall do
It might be better just to take your hand and try to do my
   best
However feeble that may prove to be
And leave the power and the promising to you.

The guidance game

There is as much rubbish talked about guidance as there is
about any other problematic concept in the Christian world.
We talk (many of us) as though our lives are neatly punctu-
ated by a series of divine signposts erected by the Holy Spirit
at key points and crossroads. It simply is not so. I don't mean
that it doesn't happen. If God wants to give specific guidance to one of his followers, that is precisely what he does,
and always has done. On a very small number of occasions
in the course of my life, I have felt fairly confident that I am
being guided to a particular place, person or situation.

More recently my wife and I have experienced this kind
of confidence in a way that we have never known before.
Our decision to move from the south of England to Scargill
House in North Yorkshire in 2009 was an extraordinary
experience. In the previous year, we felt we had reached
a crossroads in our lives, and we asked God to make it clear
if he had a specific plan for us. We decided to accept no

speaking invitations for 2010, and then we waited. Some weeks later we began to hear about the 'death' of Scargill, and the possibility of a resurrection. From that time onwards there were no messages in the sky, and no ambiguous coincidences, just a powerful and absolute assurance that God wanted us to be there. We moved to Scargill in August 2009, and the Centre reopened early in 2010.

Incidentally, confidence in our location doesn't stop us screwing up, but at least we can be sure we are screwing up in the right place. What were we called to? There is not enough space here to talk about all that God has done since the Centre reopened, but a poem that Bridget and I wrote early in our stay conveys the general ethos of the place quite well, and hints at the way in which our guests are invited to spend healing time in a world that offers laughter, love and permission to be themselves. We have not attempted to create a new world at Scargill: rather, we have tried to create the best possible framework for the Holy Spirit to occupy and work in.

Blessed is Scargill

Blessed are the puzzled barns, the frowning scars, the gills,
The endless over-arching sky, the rain tormented hills.
Blessed are the toddling, tombstone sheep,
Counted by the shepherds in their waking hours,
As well as in their sleep.

Blessed are the swallows and the martins and the bats,
The weasels and the foxes and the pheasants and the rats.
Blessed are the partridges, the curlews and the voles,
The buzzards and the bluetits and the blessed, blinking
  moles.

Blessed are the rabbits,
Blessed are their overactive reproductive habits
Blessed are the farmers, who adore the bunnies too,
Under pie-crust, or with dumplings in an unforgiving stew.

Blessed are our neighbours and our churches and our pubs,
Our singers and our ringers, all our cafés and our clubs.
Blessed are the buses and twice blessed when they stop,
Blessings upon blessings on our local village shop.

Blessed are the garden walls,
Where morning peach and evening purple falls,
Upon the soft seclusion of that magical retreat,
So secret, so sweet.

Blessed is this house of peace, each brick and tile and
    slate,
Each cup and bowl and jug and spoon, each knife and fork
    and plate.
Blessed is the altar, blessed are the pews,
Blessed are the bedrooms, thrice, quadruple blessed are the
    loos
Blessed are the doors, the floors, the neverending daily
    chores,
The mains, the drains, the window panes
Blessed is the bravely futile chapel damp-defier,
    someone's tiny, optimistic dehumidifier.

Blessed are the visitors,
The short, the tall, the sensitive, the numb,
The ones who sadly shake their heads and wonder if their
    turn will ever come
Blessed are the blighted, blessed nuisances,
The ones who make us tear our hair,

And swear, and punch our pillows in the middle of the
    night,
Blessed is the sane and gentle light that warms the heart of
    true responsibility.

Blessed are the fat, the thin, the straight, the bowed, the bent,
Blessed are the ones who book, and blessed are the ones who
    reach our doors by some strange accident.

Blessed are the lost, the bossed about,
Tired, fired, wild and wired, bullied, disappointed,
    uninspired,
Blessed is the child inside, lying low, but still wide-eyed,
And ready for a fairground ride with Jesus.

Blessed are the ones who built and loved and toiled within
    this little world of work and prayer,
Blessed is the future they have placed into our care.
Blessed are the loyal volunteers,
Who cried hot tears because they feared this home from
    home had died,
But found there was a space for them,
A necessary place for them to love it back to life.

Blessed is the playground, and the laughter that at last,
Will ripple through this valley like an echo of the past

Blessed – all our hopes and dreams, the planning and the
    visions,
Blessed are the difficult decisions.
Blessed – this community,
Resurrected, newly born, restored.
Blessed are the Yorkshire Dales
Blessed is the Lord.

Common sense and the Holy Spirit?

What about Jesus and guidance? Well, first of all, he didn't screw up, as Bridget and I do on a regular basis, but he does seem to have pursued his ministry on a need-to-know basis. The Bible tells us that he was shocked, frustrated, amazed and driven to anger at various times. These are not the emotions of a person who is privy to all things, even though he was truly God as well as truly man. Of course, much of the time he knew exactly what was happening and what was going to happen, especially when, as the Bible puts it, he was filled with the Spirit.

What about us? Perhaps we expect too little and too much. I believe it is irrational to expect that Christian lives patched together with the flimsy thread of coincidence will yield much in the way of authentic guidance, but all of us can be filled with the Holy Spirit, and that is probably what we should be praying for. In the end, however, it is God who decides when we need specific leading, and it's up to him to make it available at those times. In the meantime we have to get on with it. Stay close to God in prayer, make good, common-sense decisions, and ask for the Holy Spirit to stop you if you make a wrong turning. Get on with it. Take responsibility. There are too many people doing nothing because the divine oracle has not spoken.

There are good, useful questions to be asked on this subject. What are my experiences of guidance, if any? Was it God, was it me, or was it too much cheese eaten last thing at night? Do I really want guidance, bearing in mind that God might reveal my destiny as drinking gin and tonic in the Ritz, or living in squalor among people who need me, or just about anything in between? Should

I pray to be filled with the Holy Spirit? What does that mean to me? Be careful. Remember my continually recurring piece of advice – you never can trust God.

Guidance, the sacred cow that can lead you into a ditch

Still on this subject, a young man wrote to me a few years ago, expressing his worries about God and guidance. He seemed to have become almost paralysed by fear and uncertainty connected with this issue. I would guess that the problem arose from the fact that on the planet inhabited by most of the Christians he knew, guidance was available like some sort of divine sat-nav. You always knew where to go and what to do next because the voice of the Holy Spirit kept up a detailed description of the ideal route, rather like one of those rally-car co-drivers. On Sam's planet that was not the case. Helpfully, I knew Sam's planet well. I live there. This is the letter that I sent him. It would be good if some of the folk on that other planet could pick it up on one of their sophisticated communication systems.

Dear Sam,

Thank you for your interesting letter. If you are nuts you are certainly my kind of nuts. I understand all that you say about getting into a neurotic state about going with or against God's will because I used to be almost as bad myself. I seem to have settled down a bit nowadays. I think a major breakthrough was the realisation that there is quite enough very clear guidance in the Bible without me getting myself into a state about all the stuff that isn't. By that I mean that I don't actually need any

specific guidance to inform me that I should not steal
from Boots, or that I should be nice to my children, or that
I should do my best to forgive people who hurt or annoy
me, or that I should avoid committing adultery or any of
the rest of the long list that can be assembled from all the
teaching we find in the New Testament. You mention the
fact that you and your charming and long-suffering
fiancee have problems with your physical desires. It
would be very disturbing if you didn't, but, tough as it
might be, you are clearly well aware of what is a good
idea and what is not a good idea in that respect, so there
is no confusion over guidance as far as things like that are
concerned.

That is one point.

The second point is about Paul the apostle. This
extraordinary man tells us that he prayed constantly and
had a serious desire to be in the centre of God's will. You
may recall that he and his fellow-travellers made an
attempt to enter a place called Bithynia, but the Spirit pre-
vented them. Paul had made a good, common-sense decision about going to this place, and it was not an enraged
thunderbolt that stopped him, but a practical, helpful
instruction from the Holy Spirit.

Jesus clearly operated on a need-to-know basis when it
came to guidance. The Bible says that there were times
when Jesus himself was obliged to take a different direction from the perfectly reasonable one that he had
embarked on. The point is this. Most of the time we are
not going to be given direct, specific guidance from God.
As long as we are staying close to him in prayer and in
obedience to the things that we *do* understand, then we
can get on with our lives, confidently making intelligent,
loving decisions, in the knowledge that if he wants us to
stop, or change our direction, or go back to where we

started, then he will make it clear. And that brings me to my third point.

As far as I can see, neither Jesus nor Paul ever operated or changed their plans on the basis of a feeling that the Lord might possibly be saying that they might be right to do something or other. This is modern-church speak, and I think it is nonsense. Why in the name of thingamabob would God deal out wafty little half thoughts like deliberately tricky exam questions in order to resolve issues that are so important to the individuals concerned? He wouldn't and he doesn't. No, you get on with it, and remember that the initiative for guidance is God's, not yours. Better to do a thing faithfully without any particular leading, than to be drawn aside by mental and emotional vagaries that have no spiritual authenticity. I know there are people who talk as though they are in the habit of having a meticulously detailed chat with God over coffee every morning, but most of us do not.

Aslan will turn up from time to time, either silhouetted against the sky on a distant hillside, or just behind your right shoulder when you least expect him, or suddenly walking quietly beside you when you feared that you were alone. Value these times and store them in your heart, but don't see lions where there are none.

All the very best to you, Adrian

God became Chatty man

One sacred cow that really does need to be slaughtered in my opinion (don't start – it's a metaphor!), is the idea that there's something wrong with using normal human language to discuss issues of faith. There's quite a lot about that in this book, simply because it is so very important.

God became man. He didn't become a collection of weird and inaccessible patterns. Here are two ordinary people chatting about faith. Both 'A' and 'B' are Christians, 'A' quite recently converted. They could be any age from mid-twenties upwards. They get on very well, and share a similar sense of humour. 'A' really wants to know, and 'B' is determined to be truthful and unrepentantly normal.

What's the Holy Spirit?

A : This is so good of you. I'm ever so grateful.

B : Oh no, no, I'm more than happy to help if I can. When I became a Christian I never really got round to asking about all the things that were on my mind. I wish I had.

A : Why didn't you?

B : (*sighs*) I don't know, I was young. I suppose everyone else seemed to know all the answers and I thought I'd look a bit of a divvo if I kept saying, 'What about this? – don't understand that – are we *supposed* to behave like creatures from the planet Zog? – if everything God created is good, who's responsible for Benny Hinn's hair?' Sorry, that one's very silly.

A : No, don't worry, I like silly.

B : (*with gusto*) Good! Hang on to that whatever you do. I promise you'll need it. No, loads of things bothered me. I quite envy you becoming a Christian a bit later in life. You just ask questions. It's great! I'm just worried I won't have good answers. (*tentatively*) So, do you think you're beginning to get the hang of the Trinity after our last chat?

A : I think so. Well, anyway, I know what it's not. It's not like one of those Hoovers that sweeps as it beats as it cleans. Right?

B : Right. It's not one person doing three things –

A : But it is one person who's also three separate people.

B : Clear as mud?

A : Yep! And when Christian things are clear as mud, we call them 'mysteries' and move on quickly. Have I got that right?

B : Brilliant! You'll be pope by next Wednesday. Now, where did we get to?

A : Well, after last time, I think I get the 'Father' bit. My dad was lovely, and –

B : Huh! Want to swop?

A : – and God is even lovelier, so that's all right. Sorry about yours. And Jesus is the reason I signed up. He ambushed me. Looking forward to getting to know him better. Now, we didn't talk about the Holy Spirit. What's the Holy Spirit?

B : *Who* is the Holy Spirit?

A : Sorry – *who* is the Holy Spirit?

B : Well, the Holy Spirit is the one who's actually with us, doing all the – all the God stuff here on earth. Jesus told his disciples he had to go back to heaven so that the Holy Spirit would be able to come and live inside us. The Holy Spirit is Jesus, but he's also *not* Jesus. Do you see what I mean?

A : No. Do you know what you mean?

B : (*considers*) Er, no.

A : Weird. Does anyone know what it means?

B : (*solemnly*) No, it's a mystery.

A : (*pause*) Okay. Moving on. What else does the Bible say about the Holy Spirit?

B : Oh, lots of things. (*suddenly remembering*) For instance, in Paul's epistle to the Ephesians –

A : Is that the one just before the gynaecological epistle?

B : What?

A : The gynaecological epistle. Paul's epistle to the Fallopians.

B : (*mock-reproachful pause*) For instance, in Paul's epistle to the Ephesians there's something about being filled with the Spirit instead of getting drunk.

A : That's interesting. Feels a bit the same, does it?

B : Well, actually, yes, it does a bit (*realising the implication*) – I would imagine.

A : So, God's against alcohol, is he?

B : I don't see how he can be. He's responsible for hundreds of thousands of people lining up in church every Sunday morning to drink wine. And Jesus once turned gallons of water into wine at a wedding where they'd run out. His first miracle. Some Christians don't like it, though.

A : I know, I've met some of them. Nearly put me off for life. They seem to think he should have transformed it into Shloer, or better still turned the original wine into water, then they'd have run out of wine before anyone had a chance to drink any. What are those people all about?

A & B : (*pause*) Moving on . . .

B : I'll tell you something else. Whenever people get filled with the Spirit, amazing things happen.

A : Filled with the Spirit?

B : Yes.

A : (*slowly*) Filled - with a person?

B : Well, yes. The Bible talks a lot about Jesus being filled with the Spirit, and every time that happened there were all sorts of miracles, or something really important got said. Sometimes the Holy Spirit gives you words when you don't know what to say.

A : (*shakes head in silent puzzlement*) So, you tell me – not what anyone else says, not what the Bible says – for you, what's this Holy Spirit like?

B : (*thoughtfully, almost dreamily after a reflective pause*) He's kind. And wise. Shocking sometimes. Ingenious. (pause) Best of all, he finds a way when – when you've almost lost hope . . . (buries face in hands)

A : (*quietly placing a hand on B's shoulder*) Thank you.

Reproductive miracles?

Sex is not a sacred cow. Rather, it is the assumption that we really don't need to reveal or examine the issues and problems that can afflict Christians in this area.

Sometimes I flippantly ask my Christian audiences if any of them are interested in sex. One or two hands might be raised, usually by women. What a lot of little fibbers the rest of them are. Outsiders could be forgiven for wondering how Christians ever manage to have babies. Surely some sort of sexual encounter is necessary for this to happen. Perhaps I'm just not aware of thousands of reproductive miracles happening every day in the evangelical universe.

I suppose the problem is that, as usual with the way we Christians approach issues of this kind, we take the subject of sex far too seriously and not seriously enough. I am not for one moment suggesting that a succession of dirty jokes would help the situation, but I do know from experience that people can find liberation and a more relaxed perspective when a little humour and honesty are added to the equation. Simply to know that most of us are in the same leaky boat can be hugely reassuring.

This is especially helpful to those of us who have been trapped in little prisons of fear that we are the only ones enduring the tumultuous passion of sexual confusion or temptation. I recall commenting at a Bible-study group that I had rarely seen anything more erotic than Jacqueline du Pre playing Elgar's cello concerto on a television programme recorded in the Sixties. You could have cut the atmosphere with an ice-pick.

Relaxation in discussion of this area of our lives will hopefully make it easier to tackle the crucially serious aspects of sexual misbehaviour. God hates adultery and, believe you me, there's a lot of it about in the church. People need to be helped. That includes the tempted, the victims of other people's indulgence, and the church itself, which is invariably injured by moral malfunction in any part of its body. God is very nice until he stops being very nice. Think on. There are some seriously important questions to be asked. Are people scared of talking about sex? If so, why? Do you think Jesus was sexually tempted, and how did he deal with it? Why do you think people, including Christians, occasionally jettison most of the good things in their lives in order to pursue an adulterous relationship? Is it just about sex, or is it more complex than that?

The trouble with being good

While we're talking about sex, let's think about 'being good'. Is that one of our Christian sacred cows? In its pale, diluted, harmless form, I think it is. Sterile morality is so boring.

Being good for no reason other than a sort of general feeling that's it's a good thing to be good – that's not very good, is it? Why bother? I've been thinking deeply about this for many, many minutes, googling my own mind on the subject, as it were. Do have a go at that, by the way. Occasionally you find a couple of nuggets among the dross. Anyway, here's what I thought.

It is fashionable nowadays to ridicule and make jokes about those television programmes in which patently inadequate people are lured, presumably by the promise of posh hotel rooms and abundant expenses, onto a stage in front of a studio audience. They are then roared at angrily when they have the effrontery to display the symptoms of their inadequacy. A frequently repeated joke describes our more unsalubrious seaside towns as 'holding pens for *The Jeremy Kyle Show.*'

A fairly common view of this alarming contemporary appetite for programmes in which ordinary people get very upset is that their victims are distressingly shallow and often morally reprehensible. It distresses me to admit that it is a view I have rather lazily shared in the past. I repent. I really do. Recently I have begun to understand that the problem is not one of shallowness: it is one of waste. The real tragedy is that people who might have explored the fascinating depths of their own human potential are skittering around on the surface of experience, before spiralling down into a glum acceptance that grey is the true and unvarying colour of all things.

Perhaps it begins with failure to grasp the deceptive and destructive effects of instant gratification. Some of the relatively young people who appear on programmes like this have already fathered or given birth to two, three or even, in one case, four children, each conceived with a different person. Many of the explosively emotional public arguments so beloved of the programme makers have at their heart the question of whether husbands, wives, boyfriends or girlfriends have been unfaithful to their partners. Incredibly, lie detector tests are administered in order to restore trust in relationships. Faintly ironic, wouldn't you say?

It is as though the sexual act is indulged in as one might indulge in a succession of cream cakes, and please, let's not be hypocritical about this. Many people, Christians included, who would consider themselves to be sensible and disciplined in their behaviour, are all too familiar with the impulse, if not the gratification. And I'm not just talking about cream cakes.

The fact is, though, that the unrestrained consumption of squishy confectionery and indiscriminate sexual promiscuity have something in common. Both might provide a sense of instant satisfaction, but they also militate against the development of the kind of fitness, physical on the one hand, and moral and emotional on the other, that will ultimately allow a richer and more genuinely rewarding discovery of what it means to function as a complete human being.

I can almost hear some readers classifying this statement as the typically resentful ravings of someone who has reached an age where over-indulgence in just about anything causes physical or moral indigestion, but it's actually much more than that. Jesus came to bring us fitness, to benevolently shock us sometimes with the rich complexity and potential for enjoyment that already resides in the people that we are.

And of course it's not just cream cakes and sex. I know a man who was in prison for years. Apparently ineradicable, terribly destructive habits of violence and resentment ruled his life. He cried out to God, and found to his amazement that within him were the dormant mechanisms of goodness and compassion. He embraced these things and his life changed.

There was a young woman who had known only rejection and bitterness through her childhood and teenage years. She was filled with the Holy Spirit one morning (you would have to ask her exactly what she means by that) and it was as though something dark and dreadful was flushed from her system.

In both of these cases problems certainly did not totally disappear, but they began to be tackled in a context of hope and optimism.

I have to say that, in my case, the process of transformation seems to be taking an awful long time, and there are times when I get very low, but I cannot (and do not want to) lose awareness of a bright and mysterious horizon that beckons and attracts me more than the seductive trivia that surrounds us in this age.

And, in the end, that is why it is a good idea to be good, if that's what we really want to call it. We are definitely not called to sterile morality, but to an ineffable, multilayered happiness that is rooted in commitment to the will of God, and it is precisely how we human beings were always supposed to be.

When the Israelites were trekking through the wilderness God gave them a complex set of rules to live by, not because he likes rules, but because he knew exactly what was needed for successful desert survival. In the New Testament we are given spiritual teaching and guidelines, not in order to oppress and repress us, but to put us on the road to the surprising joy of true authenticity.

And that, I'm sure you'll agree, is good.

Nine

Uniting our inner world with our public one

Now we need to talk about our personal War Of The Worlds. How can we safely allow our inner world to collide or bump gently against our outer one?

This battle for authenticity in the church is on – at least, I hope it is. What do I mean? I thought you'd ask me that. I suppose I mean that the corporate voice of the church offers pronouncements and clarion cries of such seamlessly formal positiveness that the ordinary Christian, struggling with the untidiness of daily living, is more likely to be discouraged than otherwise. I have spent the last few years tediously bleating on about the fact that there are two main truths that we should be passing on to people.

One is the truth about us. This is the ragged, uncertain truth about lives that swing from faith to doubt, from ecstasy to despair, from clarity to obfuscation, from obedience to deliberate sin. Some of us do better than others, but all fall short of getting it half right, let alone aspiring to the glory of God.

The second truth is about God. God is the Father we never had, or like the father we did have, only even better. He is the source and meaning of all love. He loves us and he wants the very best for us. Because of this, he sent his Son Jesus, so that we could come home to him eventually. His ways of working in this world are filled with mystery and strangeness, whatever anyone says, but we can learn to trust him with the most important part of ourselves, the part that will live with him forever.

We leave out either of these truths at our peril if we truly desire to pass on the Gospel of Jesus. God is not looking for wonderful Christians. He knows better. As we have already seen, what he needs is obedient failures. The book of Malachi talks about the displeasure of God when we present him with unworthy sacrifices, but there is one imperfect sacrifice that he will receive with joy. Us. Whatever we are. Exactly as we are. Ready to go.

This may seem like the good news and the bad news all rolled up in one. Well, yes it is, and the business of living it out is far from easy. Where exactly can we be truly honest about our lives? How do we feel about this business of the public and private faces of our Christianity coming face to face? Will they recognise each other? And does my imperfect self really qualify for service in the Kingdom of God? One more question. How might a church work towards greater personal authenticity for its members?

These questions could be debated forever, but every now and then you come across someone who is having a good shot at becoming authentic. Take my friend Steph, for instance, the chaplain at Scargill House. I have grown to truly love Steph, not because she is perfect (I would never insult her with that sort of nonsensical claim), but because, as well as having many talents and skills, she is a kindhearted, ranting, rueful survivor who has set the compass of her heart towards Jesus. When Steph was licensed in the Scargill House chapel a while ago, I wrote this little rhyme to read during the service.

Stephanie

Stephanie prays on the pathway
Shielding her eyes from the sun
Lord, be my light for the future
Transfigure the things I have done
Fill me with courage and power
When devilry must be defied
And encourage me please to get on my knees
When shoelaces need to be tied

Stephanie stares in her mirror
A lifetime of losses and gains
She can hardly believe the image she sees
The beautiful girl who remains
Now she can open her arms to the world
And see the impossible birth
Of a sparkling surprise, a trembling surmise
That Jesus is walking this earth

Stephanie prays at the foot of the cross
My commitment is troubled but true
All that I am is all that I have
But I offer it freely to you
Father, I love you, I will do my best
But sometimes I fail and cry
Promise, when I reach the edge of myself
Your Spirit will help me to fly

The hooter's about to go!

Steph is certainly one of those people who are continually finding their inner world squaring up to their outer world and loudly challenging each other to a fight. This is not particularly surprising as she is a person of such contrasts. And there are times when those disparate elements remind me of two extremely famous sisters who, together with their brother Lazarus, probably knew Jesus as well as anyone on earth. Their Bethany home was clearly one of the few places where he could relax and be himself, assuming he managed to work out who that was, given his uniquely complex identity.

We know little about Lazarus. He was famous mainly for being dead, and then, miraculously, not being dead. The personalities of Mary and Martha, however, are revealed with unusual clarity, particularly through an incident that occurred while Jesus was visiting. Amazingly, this domestic icon of an event is related in only five verses of Luke's gospel.

> As Jesus and his disciples were on their way, he came to a village where a woman named Martha opened her home to him. She had a sister called Mary, who sat at the Lord's feet listening to what he said. But Martha was distracted by all the preparations that had to be made. She came to him and asked, 'Lord, don't you care that my sister has left me to do the work by myself? Tell her to help me!'
>
> 'Martha, Martha,' the Lord answered, 'you are worried and upset about many things, but only one thing is needed. Mary has chosen what is better, and it will not be taken away from her.'

An intriguing story. Out of the great religious jumble sale of the centuries we hear Jesus saying that only one thing is needed. Quick, let's work out what it is so that we can solve all our problems. Well, it appears to be willingness

to sit at the feet of Jesus and listen to his voice. Easy?
Maybe. We'll come back to that.

People sometimes classify individuals by describing
them as behaving like a 'Mary' or a 'Martha'. Broadly
speaking, I suppose they mean that Marys are rather
limp, wafty, usually impractical spiritual types, while
your average Martha is a pan-clashing, floor-scrubbing
straight-talker, with a heart of gold.

Bearing in mind these stereotypes, I have been fascinated by what happens when I ask people in groups to
say if they would rather be a Mary or a Martha. The first
surge of popular opinion is usually towards Mary. After
all, she chose the 'better thing', and we do all want to get
the spiritual stuff right, so that must be the way to go,
surely?

However, shortly after this slightly uneasy conclusion
has been reached, a mild panic sets in. What does it mean
to sit at the feet of Jesus when he is not physically present? Might it not be safer to get on with activities that can
be clearly measured in terms of completion and achievement? In any case, when we stop kidding ourselves, we
all know (come on, we do!), that manual work and physical effort must be more profitable and pleasing to God,
than sitting around like Lydia Languish, making daisy
chains and reading Patience Strong. Eventually, like a
zebra scenting a lion, most of the assembled company
begin a nervous stampede towards the safety of the
Martha camp, and there they huddle, happily compiling
lists of things that need to be done.

Abruptly switching metaphors, I am reminded of a
long defunct television programme called *Runaround*, featuring a quiz in which twenty or thirty children were
asked a question, and had to sprint across a large open
space to line up below one of three possible answers on

the far wall. When a hooter sounded they were allowed one chance to swop lines if they wished. The psychology was interesting. If most children lined up initially behind one of the answers, there might be a mass migration as the hooter sounded, especially if a significant percentage of the group changed position with sufficiently infectious confidence.

Mary or Martha? The hooter's about to go . . .

In churches and other Christian communities, there can be serious problems in this area. Here, as in other centres of this kind, a gap can open between 'ministry' teams and those responsible for practical tasks, such as cooking or cleaning. Each side can feel resentful about being misunderstood or unappreciated. A bunch of arty-farty Marys ranged against a phalanx of bad-tempered Marthas, that's how bad it can feel at its worst.

It happens in families. My friend Arnold had two sons. One was a dreamer who lived mainly in his imagination, and was continually surprised and perplexed by the demands of a world that existed somewhere outside his head, and another who filled his stern days with making and fixing and building all sorts of things. In their early teenage years, the boys nearly killed each other from time to time, although, as far as I know, they never hit upon the idea of calling each other Mary or Martha by way of an insult.

In the end, of course, we must jettison the more ridiculous caricatures, and learn to appreciate those who are not made like us. Marys might make a little more effort to love and value their Marthas, and Marthas might have a shot at being Marys for a while, if only to learn that there is more than one kind of hard work. The crucial point, though, is that since the Holy Spirit came, there is no hierarchy in Christian service. As my friend Steph has discovered, we can sit at the feet of Jesus whatever we are doing, whether it's cleaning toilets, preaching in Canterbury Cathedral or anything else. And we should do exactly that. In the final analysis, as Jesus clearly states, we don't need anything else.

Do I belong?

A war of the worlds rages in many people as they literally or figuratively approach the communion rail. Have I confessed enough of my sins? Have I forgotten some that would make all the difference? Will God be angry with me if I have the cheek to approach him now, after a week in which I have behaved so badly? What does Paul really mean when he talks about taking communion unworthily? Might I be about to eat and drink damnation to myself if I take the bread and wine? Doesn't the Bible say something about getting sick if you take communion when you shouldn't? Do I actually belong, or did I never make a real commitment to Christ?

The following lines, used in a communion service, are an attempt to free troubled souls from the sense that private concerns have no place in the open space where we eat bread and drink wine in remembrance of Jesus. Does it work? I think so. Do any of them fit the way you are thinking?

Do this in remembrance of me

I love and worship you as much as I ever did, and I look forward to receiving the symbols of your Son's body and blood. Thank you so much for letting me come.

I am deeply embedded in sin, and I feel that you have wasted your Son's body and blood on me. I would like to start again. Can we? Please let me come.

My faith has gone. I am in the dark. I have finally faced the fact that you do not exist, and that I have wasted half of my life on something that means nothing. And yet – I still want to come. May I?

I am so angry with you. And you know why. You know everything. Why have you let me down? You could have done *something*! A half-decent earthly father would have done ten times as much. You don't love me. Do you? I so need to come.

My life is a monument to mediocrity. I have not stirred myself to follow you into the places where I could have done something useful. It's all so lazy and thin and dried up. When I come, please wake me and feed me. Share one of your dreams with me. Show me how to help you make it come true.

I am frightened – just so very frightened. Please take my hand and look after me as I come.

I am confused. So much debate. So many words. Too many words. I say far too many myself. Please meet me in this buzzing headache of a cloud. I am coming to you. I need to find peace in your words or your silence.

I am so tired – so very tired. Near to giving up. I think you know the feeling. Remember me as I do this in remembrance of you.

I am worried, worried, worried. Some say I should leave my burdens behind when I come to you. I cannot. So – is it all right for me to come up to you with my burdens? They're going to stand awkwardly around my feet like a week's shopping from Morrisons, but I will make sure that my hands are free. Let me come.

I'm not coming for me. I'm coming for you. You asked me to drink wine and eat bread in remembrance of you. Thank you for inviting me, and forgive me for thinking only of myself. Of course I'll come.

Promising treats

At Scargill House community members make promises according to a Pathway of Life devised and written soon after the conference centre re-opened. It involves promises to do our best to follow the example of Jesus in various areas. Interestingly, many people have trouble with this.

'Surely,' they say, 'community members should commit to obeying a rule, rather than promising to do their best? Isn't that a bit of a cop-out?'

Role-playing patient willingness, I explain that, actually, doing your best is more demanding and less constricting than making huge promises that you will never keep. Christians are all too familiar with the pattern of publicly promising the earth and delivering Hartlepool. Not, I hasten to add, that there's anything wrong with Hartlepool – as far as I know. I've never been there, but I'm sure it's beautiful. It's just not the whole earth.

Anyway, the point about community members promising to do their best is that praise and discipline relate to the individual, rather than some formulaic measurement of behaviour that ignores effort and progress. Thus, person A, who could have lost his terrible temper four times in one week, might have limited it to two, and would deserve congratulations. Meanwhile, person B, diseased with sarcasm, has caused havoc with her indulgent behaviour and needs stepping on – in love.

Some promises are scary, like the one about doing our best to follow the example of Jesus in remaining 'obedient to the point of crucifixion'. We are not expecting our members to suffer in that way (I hope) but the bar is set by the Master, and the spiritual Fosbury Flop demanded from us plodding followers of Jesus is simply the highest we can reasonably manage.

Not all our promises are that challenging. The Scargill Council vetoed our attempts to include a commitment to sometimes being 'silly' (not that this will prevent us being strategically silly from time to time, of course), but we retained the essential element of giving treats, expressed like this:

We see Jesus taking great pleasure in receiving and giving unexpected treats to other people.
Yes! With God's help, and with encouragement and guidance from the brothers and sisters who share this pathway, we promise to try our very best to follow the example set by Jesus.

What a wonderful promise to make! Not just giving, which is fun, but taking as well. And if you want reassuring back-up from Scripture, consider that magical moment when a woman looked into the eyes of Jesus and saw a person worn out with service to others. Generously, she treated him to her most valuable possession, a jar of precious ointment that calms and balances the nerves, and must have cost the equivalent of almost a year's wages. He gladly took it. And he loved it. And he loved her for giving this treat to him. Here is a somewhat dramatised version of that event.

The woman with the ointment

He looked up after a moment or two and stared at them with a funny expression on his face. It seemed to me a mixture of weariness and scepticism and anger.

'Well,' he said, 'you'll be pleased and relieved to hear that your huge and somewhat surprising enthusiasm for feeding the poor will certainly never be wasted. I mean,you're going to have them with you for ever. That's the good news. So, you'll be doing something for them today, will you? Or tomorrow perhaps? I'm not preventing you from getting on with your good works, am I? I would hate to hold you up. As for me – well, for better or worse or both, you won't have me with you for very much longer. Not very much longer.'

A sort of shiver ran right through his body when he said that, and when he went on speaking, his voice was much softer, much more gentle. I'm not sure, but I think there were tears in his eyes. I think it was probably because someone had done something for him for once.

'And this – this thing that she has done is so – so different. It is quite simply one of the most generous, beautiful things that has happened to me in a very long time, and I am going to really enjoy it. There is no actual virtue in misery, believe it or not. So, you go and feed the poor and leave this dear woman alone. Just leave her alone. She has freely given me the most valuable thing that she had, and I am most grateful.'

'You mean the oil of spikenard?', they asked.

'Oh, you really, really don't understand, do you? No, the ointment is wonderful, but what she has given me today is far more valuable than any scented oil could ever be.'

He turned and looked her straight in the eyes.

'Thank you so much for understanding my poverty, and for feeding me. Not many do that. A note has been made in heaven, you know. No-one there or in this world will ever forget you, and that includes me.'

By the way, there are parallels to family life in this business of giving treats according to individual levels of achievement. Bridget and I had three sons and one daughter. Certainly, it made sense to encourage them to do their best according to their lights, instead of pushing towards a universal benchmark achievable by one or two but not by the others. In matters of behaviour, there were times when a very small step forward needed to be acknowledged and sometimes rewarded, so that more progress could be made. The downside of this, as all weary parents know, is that cries of 'It's not fair!', and 'How come he's allowed to get away with that when I'm not?' become a part of everyday life. Never mind. We survive.

I honestly think that all my memories of treats are good ones. There is something piquantly, refreshingly exquisite about giving or receiving treats that are unexpected and undeserved. Looking even further back than my children's early years, I recall, as though it was yesterday, my mother meeting myself and my brother at four o'clock outside the gates of the junior school and announcing that we were off to watch *Davy Crockett* at the Essoldo Cinema in Tunbridge Wells. Wonderful!

There were always lots of treats as our kids were growing up. Toys, sweets, walks, picnics, games, staying up late, getting up early, watching plays written and performed by Matt, Joe, David and Kate, eating meals cooked and served as a surprise by the same versatile quartet, all sorts of delightful things offered and received with love.

I have to confess that one of my favourite personal memories is being almost forcibly dropped off by everyone at a country pub on Fathers' day to read the paper and eat a Sunday roast in solitude. Suited me.

Yes, horses for courses and lots of treats. That might not be how the Bible puts it, but I can recommend having a go. It warms the cockles of your heart (I'm not sure what they are, but it definitely warms them).

The Railway Children moment

When Christians are relaxed and feeling able to talk honestly, you quite often hear the same dream or yearning expressed. Something to do with wanting God to turn up in a more dynamic or unmistakeable way than in the past. A deep cry of need for a non-religious, intimate encounter with a presence rather than an implication. In this age, we are deluged with books and DVDs and songs and spoken messages that strive to plug the gap between theory and practice in the Christian life. The suggestion is that if we were to start doing *this*, or stop doing *that*, or follow a particular set of principles in the right order, then we will suddenly discover that God was there all the time, just waiting for us to get our spiritual act together. Are they right? Who knows? Surely one or two items in this library of systematic revelation must be of some use.

Where can we meet God? Where will I find the trysting place for a conversation with Jesus? In one very important sense there are as many answers to those questions as there are individual Christians. God does whatever he wants, whenever he wants, and in any way that he chooses, and we have to believe that he is an expert in the selection of times and places. Perhaps, though, there are what we might call 'gateways' to the vestibule of heaven, somewhat unexpected ones occasionally, where Jesus can sometimes be found waiting and willing to be close for a while.

There are quite a lot of these entrances, and not all of them are specifically religious ones. Music (of many different kinds, from heavy rock to Mozart, depending on what clicks your latch) is certainly one of these, and so are other forms of art. Dance, poetry, drama, film, written fiction and fine art are all, potentially, portals that will admit us to the presence of God. Excellence or heartbreaking effort in sport is another. The natural world, so rich and stunningly diverse, is yet another. Prayer, immersion in the Bible, worship of the best kind, acts of love and kindness given and received might also draw us into unexpectedly profound encounters with the God we are longing for. These things are not God, and are not to be worshipped. They are gateways to the place in our hearts where Jesus lives. That is why these words appear in the fourth chapter of the letter to the Philippians: 'Finally, brethren, whatsoever is true, whatsoever is honourable, whatsoever is right, whatsoever is pure, whatsoever is lovely, whatsoever is of good repute, if there is any excellence and if anything worthy of praise, dwell on these things.'

Immersion in beauty or appreciative emotion is not just a sort of secular bubble-bath. There is no such thing as a divine sunset, as opposed to a worldly one. Personally, my spirit revolts against these mean impoverishments of the human and Christian condition. And who knows when Jesus might decide to turn up in the centre of one of these experiences? If he does, please listen carefully to what he says.

Go and sit in a place that is good for you, and ask yourself these questions. Have you ever had a vivid encounter with God? How and where did it happen? If you have never had that kind of experience and would like to, where are you willing to look, and what are you prepared to try? And, for the benefit of all those with whom you come into contact, please ask yourself one more question. What are the merits and deficiencies of separating the so-called sacred from the so-called secular? The future of the church might depend on the answer to that one.

The walled garden

In the early spring of 2009, before the question of whether Bridget and I should move from Sussex to Yorkshire was either asked or answered in any formal sense, we travelled north to visit the Scargill estate with our good friends Phil and Di Stone. We were there for two reasons. The first was to relax and enjoy ourselves, the second was to see and feel and get as near as possible to this place, Scargill House, a place we had all visited on a number of occasions in the past. The business of 'saving Scargill', whatever that might turn out to mean, had been on our minds and in our spirits for some time. Who could tell what the future would bring? We certainly had no idea, but we had been watching every development with great interest.

There was a little gate open at the bottom of the drive, so, conveniently forgetting all we had ever known about the laws of trespass, we walked in and explored the grounds. Memories flooded back. Events, features, people, parts of the estate whose existence we had forgotten. One of these was the walled garden. How could we have forgotten that? Those huge, high, thick old walls. The profusion of shrubs and flower beds and narrow interlocking paths criss-crossing the whole area. Passing through the gate into this charming, already overgrown, private little world was like entering a mysterious, secret garden.

We sat there for a while, talking and praying and wondering what the future might hold for us all. The memory of that short time has never left me. Was the air scented with promise and prophecy? Who can tell? What I do know for sure is that my perception of that enclosed, abandoned space was very close to what I have seen in the lives of so many people who have visited Scargill since it reopened in 2010. We all have a secret garden inside us. It is our place, the part of our lives where we really live. The place where we face what we are and, rather hopelessly at times, what we are not.

Some parts of the garden are wild and poorly tended, dark and dank. We have never allowed the light to penetrate these unproductive mini-jungles. Perhaps we have been too ashamed to look at them ourselves, let alone allow strangers access to such sad corners of our lives.

Some bits are not too bad, not too bad at all: We feel quite proud that the small, emerging shoots we see there really are ours. We care for them because they bring us colour, promise hope, offer a slender confidence that all things could be well.

In our secret gardens there are walkways, ill-defined and overgrown. Once upon a time we knew where they began, how they circled round to meet the moment of our greatest need. At one time there was a well-worn path to peace. We knew it by heart and we tended it carefully. We would love to find it now, but how can we? It has been neglected for so long.

They are quite a mixture, our secret gardens, and we might feel they compare very badly with a lot of others, but we are learning to invite God in because he actually seems to enjoy being there and, although he offers constructive ideas from time to time, he never judges us or makes us feel wretched about our home, the place where we live.

Sometimes indeed, he rolls his sleeves up and gives us a hand clearing the ground for new seeds and bulbs to be planted, or cutting back the stuff that keeps the light out. That kind of work can be painful and tiring, but – well, he does seem to know what he's doing, and you learn an awful lot working side by side with an expert.

I am pleased to say that Scargill is once again becoming a place where people feel safe enough to invite Jesus into the very centre of their lives, into the secret place where things don't work out in the way that everyone says they should, where beautiful flowers and rank weeds grow within sight of each other, and many of the old familiar paths have become ill-defined.

Wouldn't it be fantastic if Scargill, and all other places that represent Jesus, were to become havens where the only law is grace, and those who are weary and confused and in need of unconditional love are allowed to allow God to put his arms round everything that they are, rather than an edited version of themselves?

It is an ambitious vision. I know that. But don't argue with me about it. Argue with the one who calmed storms by the power of his voice, and fed thousands with someone's packed lunch. It's his vision.

Rice pudding and Jesus

An intriguing aspect of this business of uniting inner and outer lives is that when you are actually engaged for and with Jesus in some simple task, however humble, the problem seems to shrink and lose its power. Bridget and I felt this once in South America when we were allowed to feed about a hundred kids with milky rice pudding out of huge metal containers, as they trooped happily out of their meeting place. There was a simple joy about performing this useful, uncomplicated job that put a smile on both our faces. So it should. Theology and real life were locked in a warm embrace for once.

The young lady in this monologue had a very similar experience.

The woman who looked after the towels

I once asked my wise father, 'Will I see change in my life?'

'Daughter,' he replied, 'one day you may live in a different village. Perhaps your task in life will alter so that the things you see and hear and touch are new and unfamiliar. That is one kind of change. There is also a change of mind and spirit. When that happens, even the most ordinary, familiar and unvarying things of life can be transfigured.'

My father's answer stayed in my heart, but I did not understand it. Until today.

I provide clean dry towels for the guests at my master's house. Today the travelling teacher named Jesus arrived with his followers to celebrate the Passover in our upper room. Imagine my amazement when, after they had eaten, the man called Jesus filled a bowl with water, knelt on the floor, and began to wash the feet of his own followers. A rabbi washing feet! Can a thing be impossible and also possible? I did not believe so until now.

Almost immediately a disagreement broke out, the largest of the disciples beating the air with his finger and declaring something in a loud voice. There was a quiet reply from the rabbi, and then the big man seemed to be begging Jesus in equally passionate tones to perform a service for him.

After that the washing continued, and finding that the cloth he had placed around his waist was very quickly sodden, the Master turned and beckoned for me to bring dry towels.

I helped him. I helped Jesus. Side by side, on our knees, we made our way from man to man. After washing the feet of each one with great thoroughness and care, he would turn to me for a towel to be placed across his outstretched hands. When the task was completed, he smiled at me and said, 'Thank you. You and I work well together, do we not?'

I could have stayed there on my knees beside Jesus for ever. And father was right. My work is different. Those I serve are different. Even the simple towel that hangs over my arm is different. I helped Jesus. We worked well together. Everything has changed.

Mothers in grace

Bridget and I were very fortunate with our mothers. If anyone ever came close to achieving a proper union between their inner and outer worlds, it was those two splendid women. Towards the end of her life, Bridget's mother, Kathleen, devoted her whole self to preserving her husband's dignity as he slipped inexorably into the dark cave of dementia. I thought of Kathleen recently while dining at a hotel in Eastbourne. The elderly lady on the next table was protecting and assisting her confused husband with exquisite, loving care. As well as reminding me of Kathleen and George, it seemed to me to reflect the persistent, meticulous love of God that moves through this world like a silent river. That night I wrote this poem.

Edward, my love

Oh, Edward, dear Edward,
Sweet light of my life,
Just spread out your napkin,
And pick up your knife.
The stars shone through velvet,
Like needles of light,
When you asked me to dance,
On the terrace that night.

Oh, Edward, not croissants,
Too flaky, my dear,
You're so good with toast,
And there's marmalade here.
Champagne and moonlight,
Lounge suit and lace,
Kisses and whispers,
Your hand on my face.

Darling, don't shout,
No, you know it's not Ted,

It's that nice man called Stephen,
Who helps you to bed.
Morning came flowing,
In silvery streams,
As my face touched the pillow,
I danced in my dreams.

I'll walk in front, dear,
You're so strong and tall,
I need you behind me,
In case I should fall.
I promised that night,
For good or for ill,
To love you forever,
And sweetheart, I will.

Time after time

People quite often ask me what I enjoy most about being a writer. I am very fortunate. There are quite a lot of answers to this question. The one that seems most relevant to *War of the Worlds*, and to this section of the book in particular, is the fact that I am able to spend much of my time getting dirty water off my chest in the form of poetry and prose. This has been the case since I first started to write, and the process has been very therapeutic for me and, as I discovered to my surprise in those early days, quite helpful for some of my readers as well. I should add, however, that this deep-cleaning effect is only possible when I don't do a moral or religious edit on the things that I produce. I certainly don't go out of my way to write gratuitously offensive material, but I do try my very best to express the contents of my heart without papering over any 'unsound' cracks. Giving myself permission to go public with the truth about myself has been refreshing, alarming and liberating. No going back now. What an act of treachery that would be.

Here is a slightly strange poem that is saturated with tentativeness and hope and mostly fear. Sometimes I lose all sense of shape and continuity in this life that I cannot escape, and feel the need to wrap it all up in words and throw it out of the window in the hope that God might catch it and glance through what I've written.

I have no idea what the first verse is about, the second is about my wife and the third is based on something that happened to me when, as a very small child, I got lost among the giant dolls' houses of Tunbridge Wells. I think the fourth verse is about Jesus.

Time

The rain has come
Garbo muslin drawn across the blemished beauty of the
     dales
Promising that all of us might be allowed to weep with
     honesty one day
The air is warm and sad and beckoning
I reach my hand out
In these heavy drops there is a softness that I never
     knew before
Kind, insistent voices call me, urge me to be brave
To fly, the moment that I hear my hour chime
With all the ragged angel wings that sweep across this
     sky.

But how shall I decide?
The rain has come
I think it might be time

My friend is here
The one I have entrusted with a scrap of paper scribbled
  over with the truth
She guards it well, as I protect her neatly written offering
But more than that, it is a Siamese attachment
A thousand miles apart, the body of our being moves in
  parallel
Connected at the heart
And now I ask myself
How will the way we are dissolve into the earth or flicker
  into space?
I shall dream a resolution if the oracles are dumb
Another night in which to lie awake or dream
My friend is here
Perhaps the time has come
A silence falls
Far more or worse than simple lack of sound, a vacuum
  of responsibility
The frozen hush I knew when I was small and lost my
  parents in a busy town
Six towering feet of silence and an empty hand
Though all around me voices speak in unknown tongues
  and rumbling giants roar
My terror traps me in an arctic well of soundlessness
Scrabbling in my panic at those icy walls
I know, I know, I know that I will not survive
I do, my parents find me in the end
Ah well, they breeze in bright relief, at least you're still alive
Now this silence falls, and I am not a child
Surely he will come if it is time

A fire is burning
Buried in its heart an overflowing treasure chest of heat
Bright shining festival of change
This glowing cache of light
Is fuelled and fed by broken, lost, discarded things
A strange transfiguration that depends on death
But cannot be allowed to die
Collect these precious golden embers
Take them now before it is too late
Use them to ignite a flame in some neglected place
A fire is burning
It is time

Just a minute

While we're on the subject of time, how much do you think can be crammed into sixty seconds? Here are some suggestions. Is what follows a great piece of literature? Well, I can't remember what the word 'sublime' actually means, and I can't be bothered to look it up, but I can confidently state that we are now taking a giant step towards the ridiculous.

In one minute

In one minute I can boil two-ninths of an egg
In one minute I can ring a friend for the best of all possible reasons – no reason at all
In one minute, as long as I am not guilty of hesitation, repetition or deviation, I can win points on *Just a Minute*

In one minute, after hearing the doorbell ring, I can, with a sixty-second burst of explosive activity, turn my study into a room that looks pleasantly untidy on the surface, but is basically well organised

In one minute I can make promises to God and mankind that will commit me to another human being for anything up to sixty years

In one minute six and a half, Usain Bolt can run approximately six hundred and seventeen metres

In one minute I can watch fifty-nine and a half seconds more of *Big Brother* than I shall ever want to see in this world or the next or anywhere else

In one minute I can find my newspaper, lose my glasses, find my glasses, lose my newspaper, put the kettle on, find my newspaper and my glasses, sit down with my newspaper and glasses and wonder why the kettle's boiling

In one minute I can grill a minute steak, a steak that, as we all know, is minute, and therefore takes exactly one minute to grill

In one minute my father-in-law chewed only one mouthful of food, with the ghost of *his* dead father standing over him counting off the number of times his jaw moved

In one minute, when a late film that I want to watch is about to begin, I can pray for my family, my church, the church all over this country, the church worldwide, the Queen, our government, everyone else's government, the poor, the rich, the lost, the saved and anybody else who comes to mind. Quite often I have a few seconds to spare at the end, which is useful if I need to get a snack ready before the film starts

In one minute I can waste one minute
In one minute I can be forgiven four hundred and ninety
   times – or more
In one minute I can read this poem. Oh, look at the time,
   no I can't . . .

When it 'appened

Now that we are nearing the end of this section, perhaps I should mention that there are definitely times when it is far better to keep your inner world inside and your outer world in a completely different place. Here is an example of that phenomenon, and you must judge for yourself whether or not the truth should have come out immediately. I really cannot decide.

It concerns George Reindorp, bishop and broadcaster, who appeared regularly on the TVS epilogue programme *Company* with Bridget and I, back in the early eighties. George was a delightful man with a wicked sense of humour, and he was a truly accomplished raconteur. The story embodied in this sketch was drawn from his experiences as a parish priest, and illustrates with disturbing clarity the kind of unexpected pressures that ministers have to endure, and the selective honesty with which some situations might need to be handled.

Parishioner : (*appearing at the front door and addressing George in a flat, monotonous tone*) Vicar, I've come straight round to tell you. It's 'appened.

Vicar : (*completely flummoxed but managing to hold it together*) Has it? Has it? Good heavens. Right. Right. Right . . .

P : Yes, it's 'appened.

V : Right, right, yes. So when exactly erm . . .?

P : About half past ten.

V : Right, so that was probably a little later than you expected, wasn't it, wasn't it, wasn't it? Was it?

P : A little bit earlier, vicar.

V : Yes, yes, of course, now you say that, it would be, a little earlier, yes, of course. So, now you're feeling   . . .?

P : (*she does a little hand balancing*) Well . . .

V : In some ways I suppose we have to say it was a bad er sad thing . . .

P : Well . . .

V : But, but, but, in a way, I expect, in a way, you know, a blessed – a blessed rel – a blessed thing.

P : Yes, vicar, but the thing I have to decide now is – should I or shouldn't I?

V : Right, right, right – well, I suppose, you know, we have to bear in mind that this may not be the ideal time to make, you know, those big decisions, not immediately after er . . .

P : Well, it's not really a *big* decision, is it?

V : Well, not a – not a *big* decision, no, in that sense. But, I mean, it's not a tiny one either, is it? So, perhaps it would be better not to make it so soon after er . . .

P : After it's 'appened.

V : Well, quite, yes, quite.

P : Strange it 'appened on a Wednesday, vicar.

V : Oh, yes, yes! *Most* strange – on a Wednesday. Imagine it happening on a *Wednesday*!

P : Sorry! I mean – a Thursday.

V : Yes, I meant Thursday! Of course I did. I meant Thursday as well. Silly – er, silly me. Yes, imagine it happening on a Thursday.

P : I hope you don't mind me asking – has it ever 'appened to you, vicar?

V : To me? Er, well, perhaps not in quite the same way . . .

P : Right – and when it 'appened to you in not quite the same way – did you, or didn't you?

V : Mmmm, as far as I can remember, at first I didn't, and then – after, you know, a decent interval – well, then, I did.

P : Right. I like that. I think that's what I'll do, vicar. At first I won't, and then, after a decent interval, I will.

V : Good, good-good-good-good-good-good-good, that's good . . .

P : Did you er – did you want to come round and er have a look, vicar?

V : Do you know, I don't think I will. I think it might be best not. Because, well – I think we both know on a very deep level why that's probably not a good idea, don't we?

P : We do, vicar. Yes, we do. All right, vicar – well, thank you. I'd better get back and make sure the shed door's shut, just in case it er – you know.

V : The shed door . . . Oh yes! I do know, good gracious, yes, do I *know*?

(*At the church door some months later, on the day of the vicar's departure, and I might add that George swore this was the conversation that occurred, word for word.*)

P : I wanted to see you before you leave, vicar, to just say thank you.
V : Oh, well, thank *you*. What er – what for?
P : Well, the thing is, I'll never forget – you know, when it 'appened –
V : Oh, yes?
P : Well, you was the only one who really understood . . .
V : Ah!

Father to the man

A final reflection in this part of the book. I recently picked up and read a story that I wrote several years ago. It was called 'Father to the Man', and it appears in a collection of short stories under the same title.[3] I was shocked. When you write as much as I do, it's almost like keeping a diary. I had forgotten how agonisingly autobiographical this story was. I have no intention of further torturing myself by anatomising these connections to my past life too closely. However, at the risk of sounding completely mad, I will say that as I finished reading the narrative I cried out aloud and physically threw the book from me, in order to distance myself from the corkscrewing effect of these fictionalised memories. It was horrible. I really thought I had faced and accommodated these aspects of my life, but clearly they are still sitting inside me and are not wholly resolved. Perhaps they never will be. Perhaps they are necessary reminders. God knows. I don't.

Leaving aside these evidences of failed self-therapy, I must say that, paradoxically, I was gripped by the themes explored in the story. Most of us move onward and upward (if at all) in a spiral fashion, revisiting questions and concerns again and again, hopefully acquiring a shallow, extra accretion of understanding each time. That is true for me, although sometimes the spiral becomes a circle and there is no upward movement. Never play Swingball with the devil.

Alcohol is one theme. The story is soaked in it. I was always fascinated by Paul's advice to the Ephesians to be drunk, not with wine, but with the Holy Spirit. I have already pointed out that drunkenness is nominated by Jesus in Luke's gospel as one of three things that we should carefully avoid for the good and practical reason that they will weigh our hearts down. Presumably Paul and Jesus were aware that the effect of drinking alcohol, not even necessarily to excess, is one of the finest counterfeits dreamed up by the dark side. Good red wine and German beer are near the top of my list of the best, most delectable things the world offers, but nowadays I drink in moderation and, more importantly, I no longer believe that seductive lie about the possibility of finding peace and healing at the bottom of the very next glass. Ultimately, alcohol solves nothing. Paul, the main character in this story, is beginning to learn that.

The second main theme of the story is something to do with truth and openness in relationships. Paul withholds important areas of himself from his wife and best friend, unwilling and almost unable to risk dealing truthfully with two of the most important people in his life. Of course, there are no rules about this, but those of us who identify with such a handicap are well aware that there are times when we experience tumult or anguish or indeed a rush of positive emotion, or all three, that would be wonderfully beneficial to ourselves and those who, as Paul Tournier puts it, circle us continually like a small boat around an island, looking for somewhere to land.

This paralysis of communication causes pain, confusion, distortion and sometimes a tragic waste of shining possibilities. These challenges are daunting, but our hapless hero must tackle the problem, or face the prospect of a crippling loss.

The third theme is conversion, in this case to Christianity. There seem to be even fewer rules about this strange process, one that invariably requires us, at some point, to step into a new and often equally threatening variety of confusion and uncertainty. Measuring his image of himself against common stereotypes of church-going people is disturbing and threatening to Paul, but he glimpses a miniscule pinpoint of light in the far distance, and the path he must follow to reach it is no darker than the place in which he finds himself. The implied question at the end of the story is a predictable one. Will he complete the journey?

Writing these few lines has exhausted me emotionally. Never mind Paul. Will *I* complete the journey? Having cast a little light on my own response to this autobiographical splurge, I suppose I need to fold it all carefully into my backpack and get on with the job. Stay with me, Lord. Sometimes the truth makes my legs go weak.

Ten

The playful God

Is God playful?

Is God playful? I feel very little interest in a Christian world where po-faced gloom merchants do their best to close down the bubbling chuckles that are built into us from babyhood. As far as I am concerned, there is a war on between these two planets. Mind you, we do a fair amount of crying as well in our part of the universe. Sometimes we are too unhappy to laugh. Sometimes we are too unhappy not to laugh. Sometimes we just laugh because it feels good. And yes, I do believe that God is playful. Let me tell you about something that happened a few weeks ago.

Pears

After one of our speaking events, Bridget and I were invited to dinner with the local minister, his wife and daughter. The first course was excellent. It definitely put me in the mood for pudding, which, to my great delight, turned out to be upside down pineapple cake. At first I thought there were two of these delectable creations, but

I was wrong. The second one to land on the table was actually an upside down pear cake.

'Pears!' I cried with shamefully naked passion, 'I love pear cake! I love *anything* with pears in it. This is wonderful!'

My charming hostess was amazed, not just by my bizarrely specific enthusiasm, but also by the revelation of an unexpected connection with an experience in a local supermarket on the previous day. Intending to make an Upside Down Pineapple Cake for our Sunday lunch, she had set off down an appropriate aisle with the wholly reasonable intention of buying some pineapple.

'Buy pears,' suggested an intrusive voice in her head. 'Make an upside down pear cake instead.'

'But I don't make upside down pear cake,' she responded dazedly, 'I don't know how to do it. I don't make anything with pears. Never have.'

But the pear advocate was not to be silenced, and eventually my puzzled hostess hedged her bets by buying pineapple *and* pears. Encased in cake, these were served to us on the following day.

So, here is the question. Could it really be remotely possible that the God of Moses, Abraham, Isaac, Isaiah, Gideon, King David, Job, Jonah and Paul the Apostle had joined my friend in the supermarket one Saturday afternoon in 2011 in order to make sure that I was offered pears for pudding?

Utter nonsense? I don't think so. I think my 'pear moment' supported a growing conviction that this kind, amused God of ours is always looking for somewhere to play. This is the same God who provided good old Elijah with a little freshly-baked cake and a drink of cool water when he finally reached the end of his not very long tether, and fell into a depressed doze under a broom tree.

Do you like the idea of a playful God? How could you not?

Time for a fling

Bridget and I have been married for more than forty years or, expressed in another, rather more frightening way, slightly less than fifteen thousand days. That's a staggering number of mornings, afternoons and evenings, isn't it? Both of us would say, however, that the saga of our relationship has been well worth the time and trouble involved. We may have teetered on the cusp of killing each other on one or two occasions, but after four decades we are still the best of friends, and, generally speaking, happier in each other's company than any-where else.

Incidentally, if we reach our fiftieth anniversary I hope I shall make a better speech than the one delivered by my Lancastrian father-in-law at his Golden Wedding celebration. Rising reluctantly to his feet George removed a ridiculously small scrap of paper from the inside pocket of his suit jacket, adjusted his glasses and produced the following memorable oration.

'Well, we got married and er . . . then we had the children. And er . . . nothing much happened after that.'

That was it. That was how George summarised fifty years of married life. His wife was furious, and you can't blame her really. I'd better start planning my speech now.

Anyway, the reason I mention all this is quite simple. I've decided that after forty years, regardless of what I just said, it's time to have a fling. Other folk do it. Why shouldn't I? People would understand, I think. After all,

forty years of being with the same person doing more or
less the same thing is about as much as you can expect
from anyone, don't you think? And, let me be honest, I've
done it before. It happened one day about five years ago.
I found myself sitting on a train opposite a rather interesting looking woman. The more I looked at this person
the more I became convinced that I had met her before,
and had once known her very well indeed. Maybe this
would turn out to be a starting point for my 'fling'. Worth
taking a chance anyway. I leaned forward and spoke to
her.

'Excuse me – I hope you don't mind me asking, but
didn't we know each other a long time ago? I remember
your face *so* well.'

She gazed at me for a few moments with what I can
only describe as an exasperated expression on her face.
Then she spoke.

'Do you think you could stop talking nonsense for a
couple of minutes and pass me a sandwich?'

That's a pretty cool response for someone who's being
eyed up for a fling, wouldn't you say? Still, that's my wife
for you. The coolest of the cool.

There was a point to what I said, though. When you've
battled your way together through the long haul of bringing up four children, hardly stopping to take a breath in
the process, it comes as something of a shock when the
last one leaves and, exhausted with kidlag, you are suddenly confronted by the person you fell in love with so
very long ago. Definitely the right time to have a bit of a
fling with an old flame. And I seem to remember that that
is exactly what we did.

There is a sort of spiritual equivalent with God as well.
When Bridget and I moved to North Yorkshire there was
a real sense of adventure and reinvigoration about our

change of direction. The tectonic plates of our faith seemed to groan and shift under the pressure of divinely instigated change. As we entered the final year of our stay in that part of the world, we were more conscious than ever that the concept of having a 'fling with God' should be a familiar and welcome one in church communities. I suspect that it would do us all good to look into the face of the God who is responsible for putting us in the place where we find ourselves, remember how the love once burned, and ask what kind of a 'fling' he is planning for the future. God protect us from the tedium of flame-proof religion.

So, coming back to my desire to have yet another fling with my wife, we shall be planning our next moves (geographical and spiritual) over the coming months, and a renaissance in our personal relationship is definitely one of the moves we are planning. Looking back, I rather wish we had enjoyed a few more of these during the years that were eaten, not by the locust, but by changing, feeding, cleaning, clothing, entertaining, driving, rescuing, financing, shouting, whispering, forgiving, being forgiven, talking, listening, laughing, crying and all the other attention-consuming aspects of parenting. Like most people over sixty, we have now become experts on the things we could have done better.

As for God, well, we're trying to keep a very low profile at the moment in the hope that he'll let us stay in the north for a little while. We are unlikely to get away with it, though, and I'm glad really. It's always been the same. We know what we think we want, but when the tectonic plates start to tremble once again, I know for a fact that we shall be ready for a fling.

Is God silly?

Occasionally you hear Christians talk about humour and
laughter and plain silliness as though they are mildly
pleasant but irrelevant distractions from the real business
of following Jesus. I disagree. A man who I trust told me
an interesting story the other day. He came down one
morning to find bright golden dust all the way down his
banisters and across his living-room carpet. There was so
much that he had to sweep it up with a dustpan and
brush and throw it away. Later, he told a visitor at the
Retreat Centre where he works about this strange practical joke played by God. She was frankly sceptical, dis-
missing the whole thing as a product of imagination or
human mischief. Later that day as she was sitting on the
toilet she looked down and saw that the toilet pedestal
was surrounded by a ring of golden dust.

It does seem possible to me that, if we were brave
enough to give up religion and create real, uncluttered
space for God, there are few things he would enjoy more
than making us laugh. The name of Geoffrey Studdert
Kennedy has already popped up. Despite ministering to
soldiers in horrendous circumstances, I think he would
understand what I am trying to say about God and play-
fulness, describing, as he does, the way in which God
invariably spoilt his attempts to play fine, tragic parts
simply by laughing at him. Believe me, I know exactly
how that feels.

One thing I might have got right as a parent

When Bridget and I married forty odd years ago, we did
little planning as far as family was concerned. I suppose

we assumed we would muddle through somehow and, with God solidly on our side, it was bound to turn out more or less okay in the end. Of course, like many other childless couples, we gravely agreed on one or two specifics that never survived the arrival of real flesh-and-blood kids.

For example, our offspring, we solemnly assured each other, would never play with toy guns, because they must learn to abhor violence in all its manifestations. By the time our boys had reached the stage of rushing around yelling at the tops of their voices when we were trying to relax in the garden on our only day off, we were eagerly pressing them to take new toy guns and lots of rolls of caps down to the local recreation ground and practise violence in any manifestation that they wished. Poor parenting? Bribes? Well, yes, but it didn't half do the trick, and I have to say that despite these experiences of moral abandonment and neglect, our four children are confirmed lovers of peace.

So, did it work, our failure to put much conscious thought or organisation into ethos, standards and the rest of that very serious list? In a way it did. Children seem to absorb the qualities that are genuine aspects of their parents, whether or not there has been much analysis or forward thinking involved.

We did make lots of mistakes, me especially, but, seeing as we are talking about the playful God, please forgive me if I mention that there is one thing I might have got about right, and that was being silly. I was always quite good at that. As a family we always enjoy our little holidays from gravity and common sense, and it has done us much good over the years.

As I have already mentioned, we tried to include this requirement in the list of promises made by new members

of the community we have been part of for the last two
years, but far greater powers than us considered this a step
too far. Instead of 'being silly' we are allowed to have 'lots
of laughs'. Well, that's fair enough. We'll have lots of
laughs, and I do hope that a high proportion of them arise
through people being extremely silly.

Laughter and the sin against the Holy Spirit

Laughter can be a wonderful agent of healing on occasions. Not surprising really. It is able to have a profoundly 'normalising' effect. There are times indeed
when laughter can shock Christians, or anyone else for
that matter, into a realisation that we have been buying
into a mind-set or a world view that has very little to do
with what actually happens to real people in the real
world. Recently Bridget and I have had quite a lot of contact with folk who have endured and are still suffering
from subtle forms of bullying by so-called Christian
organisations, or individuals who have more Bible than
sense. An awful lot of this kind of thing goes on and I
hate it. People who should be looked after and protected
can so easily be crushed and made to feel guilty or bur-
dened or just plain bad. One of the most negative practices is the handing out of religious sound bites as
though the sets of words in themselves actually mean
something. Here is an example.

A man phoned me once out of the blue. I have no idea
how he got hold of my number. The dialogue went
roughly as follows:

Adrian : Hello? Adrian Plass here.

Caller : Hello, is that Adrian Plass?

A : Yes, still me. Speaking.

C : I wondered if I could ask you something.

A : Okay, go ahead.

C : (*gravely but hesitantly*) Well, the thing is – I've committed the sin against the Holy Spirit.

A : (*with bright enthusiasm*) Gosh – well done! That's quite an achievement.

C : (*with plaintive puzzlement after a surprised pause*) What is the sin against the Holy Spirit?

A : Ah, now there I can help you. I know exactly what the sin against the Holy Spirit is.

C : What is it?

A : It's stealing apples. Scrumping, they call it.

C : Scrumping? You mean –

A : Yes, stealing apples.

At this point there was an even longer pause, followed by my anonymous caller bursting into peals of laughter. So very good to hear.

What goes on in cases like this? What is it that leads apparently responsible Christian people to pull out isolated verses and fashion them into clubs for beating vulnerable people into fearful submission? You think that's putting it a bit too strongly? I don't. It's probably not strong enough, but I can never quite bring myself to be as aggressive as Jesus. Perhaps, as I grow more holy, I shall be able to manage it. I can tell you exactly what that man was wanting to say to anyone who would listen.

'I want to be loved.' That's what he and thousands of others are crying out for. It is hardly worth repeating the words of John 3:16 here because everyone knows them, but I'd better put it in anyway for newly converted ex-frog worshippers.

> For God so loved the world that he gave his only begotten son, so that whoever believes in him shall not perish but have eternal life.

And just for good measure, here is the same verse rewritten to conform with those who are busily increasing the spiritual prison population.

> For God was so graciously willing to hold his nose and put up with smelly, unattractive human beings, that he gave his only begotten son, so that all who believed in him could feel small and foolish and a bit grubby, but saved in some dull, obscure and rather disappointing way.

Laughter, love, and the occasional very straightforward telling off. These are the things that seem to work best. I commend them to you.

Eleven

The bottom line – positive crucifixion?

What is the 'bottom line', the major distinguishing feature in the world of faith that constantly wars against the planet of hollow religion? Here is a suggestion.

I was due to preach one Sunday morning at the conclusion of a weekend for unmarried folk entitled *Positively Single*. I had no hope or intention of speaking about singleness. How could I? After more than forty years of marriage, I can't even remember what it felt like to be unmarried. At the same time, the idea of being positive in various complicated situations interested me.

I came up with something to talk about in the end, but only after a typically 'silly' spell. What is wrong with me, that I cannot approach things straightforwardly? I think I must have an overactive parody gland. I wondered if we might have a weekend entitled 'Positively Sinful'. Lots of hopeful folk might sign up for that. Or how about 'Positively Adulterous'? A small group using aliases perhaps? Or we might go for 'Positively Negative'? Might as well get all the neurotics in the same room. Sorry, I do specialise in being ridiculous.

More seriously, one could run all sorts of courses for Christians with specific problems. Positively deserted, Positively distressed, Positively frustrated creatively, Positively fed up with my own dismal limitations, Positively in pain, Positively confused and unsure of what to do next. The list goes on and on.

Does this kind of spin on negative situations happen in the Bible? Perhaps. There is some evidence to suggest that it does. In the Gospel of John, for instance. One could say that Jesus was positively devastated by having to leave his friends. He points out that he must go back to his Father so that the Holy Spirit can come. Straightforward spiritual mechanics. He also tells the disciples that he needs to leave in order to prepare a place for them.

Then there is Paul. We have already looked at the way in which he was positively pierced by a thorn in his flesh. That particular weakness did allow God's strength to be made perfect, and that revelation contributed to his amazing ministry.

Mary might come to a weekend entitled 'Positively landed with the job of being the mother of the Son of God?' It can't have been easy for her to find much that was positive in most of the things that happened to her. No bed and breakfast at Bethlehem because God had spent the whole budget on angel effects. Losing her son in the Temple. The threat of a sword that would pierce her heart. That certainly happened. Mary saw the effects of a Roman flogging on her Son, and had to watch him being laughed at, racked with pain and finally dying on the cross.

So, how about the crucifixion? Now, there's something that's generally supposed to be a negative experience. And it was, of course. There was nothing light or funny about that hideous instrument of death and torture.

Crucifixion was unspeakably horrible. Perhaps we forget that. If we had to spend one Easter eating hot-garrotte-buns, we might understand and focus more clearly on the fact that we are talking about a disgusting way to die. One of my least favourite hymns is *The Old Rugged Cross*. Some find it quite moving. I don't. I am quite sure that Jesus never hankers nostalgically after that wonderful, magic day when he spent a few never-to-be-forgotten hours on the old rugged cross. Nonsense.

So, here's a foolish-sounding but serious question. Is it possible to have a positive view of crucifixion? Well, the Monty Python team had a go with *The life of Brian*, a film that was significantly helped on its way by squadrons of churchgoers campaigning against it outside the cinemas. People flooded in, presumably on the assumption that if Christians were objecting so strongly, it would almost certainly be worth watching. And it was worth watching. There are phrases from this film that will live in my memory forever.

'Blessed are the cheese-makers.'

'What have the Romans ever done for us?'

'He's not the Messiah, he's a very naughty boy.'

Slightly more problematic for many was the ditty sung by those who had been crucified: *Always look on the bright side of life*, an attempt by the Pythons to introduce a ludicrously positive aspect of crucifixion. Incidentally, I recently heard of that song being sung at a funeral service. Would Jesus have found this funny? Who knows? At the risk of being destroyed by a thunderbolt, I would have to say that I think he might.

So – the crucifixion. Could there possibly be anything genuinely positive about the crucifixion, other than the trivial fact that the death and resurrection of Jesus has made it possible for us to go home to the God who loves us more than we can possibly imagine. That's quite a positive aspect, isn't it?

But what about the crucifixion itself? How did Jesus handle that three hour experience. Here is something I find fascinating, and perhaps very helpful.

The Bible records seven things that Jesus said during that period, seven words from the cross. Here is the list:

Luke 23:34: 'Father, forgive them, for they do not know what they are doing.'

Luke 23:43: 'I tell you the truth, today you will be with me in Paradise.'

Matthew 27:46: 'My God, my God, why have you forsaken me?'

John 19:26-27: When Jesus saw his mother there, and the disciple whom he loved standing nearby, he said to his mother, 'Dear woman, here is your son,' and to the disciple, 'Here is your mother.' From that time on this disciple took her into his home.

John 19:28: 'I am thirsty!'

John 19:30: 'It is finished.'

Luke 23:46: 'Into your hands I commit my spirit.'

Amazingly, three out of the seven things spoken by Jesus in the course of this terrifyingly painful experience solved problems for other people. And a fourth one presented whole generations to come with a great gift and an immense privilege. He prayed for the forgiveness of those who were crucifying him, he comforted the man on the cross beside him and promised him a future in Paradise, amazingly, he did a bit of social engineering for his mother so that she would not be left unsupported, and he allowed us to share and take heart from that black moment when he felt alone and deserted by the one he was obeying with the sacrifice of his life.

These four cries provide key messages from the cross about Christian responsibility.

The first is a responsibility to pray to God for those who are our enemies, the ones who get up our noses, the ones who have hurt us, the ones we would rather push out of our lives. We will be held responsible for the way in which we deal with these people. No-one, least of all God, says it will be easy, but then, it never was.

Secondly, as Jesus says in the fourth chapter of John's Gospel, the harvest is plentiful but the workers are few. Wherever we are and whatever is happening to us, we should look out for those who need the 'YES' of God, because ours may be the only suffering face of Jesus that they see when everything else seems helpless.

The third message calls us to be actively loving and caring to those who are specially ours to look after: our families, our close friends, people who are practically and emotionally dependent on us.

And fourthly, we are asked to be as vulnerable and honest as Jesus about the darkness that we sometimes encounter. Remember that Jesus has been there. He doesn't ask us to walk anywhere where he has not walked himself.

The central message may be that, for followers of Jesus, being positive in the midst of difficulty, pain and frustration is not a matter of redefining the situation. There is rather too much of that going on in the church at the moment. The crap will not become positive crap when the right spin is put on it. Disaster is disaster. Bereavement is bereavement. A crucifixion is a crucifixion, and that's that. Human optimism really doesn't help either, nor does 'making the best of it', whatever that means.

No, if I want to be a truly authentic follower of Jesus, there is one main positive aspect of situations that are hurting me, if I am willing to adjust my mindset. They are mission fields. They are places in which, despite what is happening to us, we are called to watch carefully for opportunities to facilitate the specific, ingenious work of the Holy Spirit.

We cry out, 'Lord, I'm being crucified here!' And God says, 'I know. I know about crucifixion. I'm watching your back – and your soul is safe in my hands. Hold your nerve. Expect anything and everything. Help me, there's work to do.'

Whatever we are doing, wherever we are, no matter if we are in the darkness or the light, whether we are suffering or prospering in human terms, we are presented with a mission field. In wholeheartedly embracing this responsibility, I suspect that we shall be allowed to contribute significantly to ultimate victory in the battle for a genuinely Christian world.

And a final hint about that:

Poured out

We have talked about the woman who presented Jesus with that wonderful gift of precious ointment at exactly the right time. As we have seen, Jesus poured himself out even from the cross, just as that generous lady poured out her most valuable possession. The still small voice of the Holy Spirit is calling us to do the same. This was another poem originally written for The Sailors' Society.

Release the scent

Lift the lid
Release the scent
Pour the oil of care
On weariness and yearning for
A little sip, a tiny crumb of being special
Poverty of finding in the deepest, darkest place that he was sure
Of knowing if the final sacrifice would be much more than
    he could bear

Lift the lid
Release the scent
Pour the oil of peace
On troubled waters of the soul
The poverty of quietude
When lightning strikes beyond control
And fear that rolls like thunder never seems to cease

Lift the lid
Release the scent
Pour the oil of tenderness
On roughened hands outstretched to hold
The phantom forms of memory
A poverty of being told
That other, softer hands will touch and bless

Lift the lid
Release the scent
Pour the oil of fair reward
On unrelieved bewilderment
A poverty of strong support
When puzzled energy is spent
And just rebellion is a two-edged sword

Lift the lid
Release the scent
Pour the oil of being known
On loneliness and dark despair
A poverty of warm belonging
Longing for a place where breezy friendship ripples through
    the air
A place from which the black bat night of solitude has tasted
    cold defeat and flown

Lift the lid
Release the scent
Pour the oil of prayer
On unfrequented chambers of the heart
Where poverty of true completeness
Holds the parent and the child apart
And heaven dreams that one day they will be united there

Twelve

Coming home

A place to be

I would like to finish with a story about coming home. After all, home is where we shall all meet in the end.

There are certain concepts and themes that speak to the hearts of men and women in deep and special ways. Home seems to be one of these. Perhaps that is why so many people mention the parable of the Prodigal Son when asked which Bible passages are especially important to them. Many years ago Paul Tournier the Swiss doctor and author wrote a book entitled *A Place for You*.[4] In those pages he talks about this need to arrive at a destination where your heart can rest. This place, this home, might not necessarily be defined geographically. It might be a context or a group of people or an ethos or perhaps only a dream for those who have never experienced it. I believe that it is through authenticity as human beings and as Christians that we will discover the nature and location of our true home. There is a place to be, and it is very specifically for me, and for you, and for anyone else who is willing to travel. How do we get there? Thomas asked Jesus the same question after his Master announced that he would soon be going away to prepare dwelling places for his followers.

'I am the way,' said Jesus, 'and the truth, and the life.'

We shall spend the rest of our lives working out exactly how that truth can unfold, but in the meantime I shall leave you with a story. It is a strange tale, but it is definitely about coming home. See if you can work out what's going on before you get to the end of it. Good luck, and I'll see you at home, unless we meet on the way. God bless you.

Escape from the vast white plain

How could I have guessed that my exile to the Vast White Plain was destined to end in a moment of triumphant repatriation? I wish with all my heart that I had known. As it was, I suffered unspeakable agonies of pain and loss as I lay helpless and hopeless in that wretched place.

Picture my situation. I had been abandoned. For the first time in my existence I was alone. In every direction stretched a flat, utterly featureless desert of faded whiteness, surrounded on all sides by sheer cliffs of that same ghastly dead-skin colour, yet more ominously pallid in the far distance. Can pale things produce a lifeless glow? These did.

Beyond and behind those cliffs it was just possible to detect the shadowy, ill-defined shapes of monstrous, towering edifices, dark and mysterious, impossible to identify from the centre of my bleak environment.

Did I take some comfort from the fact that the light shining on me was the one I had always known? No, I did not. I could not. I was confused. Or rather, perhaps, in a state of profound shock. In the village where I belonged the sun had been a single shining orb in a sky of the brightest, balmiest blue. Here, above the Vast White Plain, the source of all light seemed to my tortured gaze to be divided or fractured into three equal and strangely shaped parts, providing incandescence rather than an outpouring of light, and offering no perceptible warmth at all.

An additional consideration. This triune sun, with no warning at all, would abruptly extinguish itself, only to reappear with equal suddenness, minutes or hours or even days later, making the Vast White Plain and the distant cliffs visible once more. How cruelly it illuminated the scene of my distress. I was accustomed to the reassuring consistency of streaming sunshine. This bizarre randomness of light and shade added to my misery. By the time my exile ended I confess that I had come to prefer the darkness.

My village. I have already mentioned my village. I was part of it. I was meant to be there. I fitted in perfectly, at least as well as any of the others. That strong sense of belonging must have contributed heavily to the deep hurt caused by my temporary rejection. I will describe the precise moment of my banishment, but first let me tell you about my village, my home, my truly delightful place of origin.

We who live there are blessed with a traditional English Village Green, complete with a small children's playground in one corner, and a pond with reeds and ducks and leafy, overhanging trees on the side nearest to our local pub, the Horse and Groom. This hostelry is a charming, ancient building with a fascinatingly uneven roof, and clusters of tall chimneys, each one uniquely shaped by the manner in which its brickwork has crumbled and worn away over the centuries.

I must be honest. You would never find me inside the Horse and Groom, but you would be right in describing me as a permanent fixture down at the end of the front garden beside the road, where two benches have been provided for village folk who love to relax and watch the world go by.

What else can I tell you? Five children, three boys and two girls, spend all their time playing happily on the Village Green. The two little girls each own a skipping rope, and the boys enjoy playing one of those eternal games of football, using the fence of the children's playground as a goal, and their colourful jumpers as goalposts. It is clear that these youngsters (they must be eight or nine years old) love the sunshine and safety of the Village Green. They are always there, just as a proud-chested little robin has staked a permanent claim to the rickety metal railing outside the Post Office, his beak opened wide as he declares that he is master of all he surveys.

There is a special parking space provided for the Post Office van, a bright splash of red, contrasting vividly with the shining emerald grass and the sky of egg-shell blue. The postman, a corpulent, cheerful looking fellow, is constantly to be seen cleaning and polishing that van of his, the only vehicle that is allowed to park beside the Green.

This central area is surrounded on three sides by beautiful, expensive residences. You only have to look at these houses to know that they are owned and occupied by the richest inhabitants of the village, those who can easily afford to buy property on the edge of the Village Green.

Ah, the edge! That word troubles me. I did harbour suspicions that those on the edge might have been the ones who initiated or somehow engineered my rejection and exile. They are so respectably straight and so closely bonded in their determination to show a bland, untroubled face to the outside world. But the rest of us are not deceived. We know that these individuals have another side to them, a side that displays as many peculiarities and idiosyncratic differences as you would find in any of us. My belief is that our varying shapes are ordained by a higher being, and therefore intended for a purpose. It would be foolish and, in a sense, ridiculously impractical to pretend otherwise.

You will understand that I am reluctant to make the following statement, but I must. An issue of colour was, in the end, responsible for my rejection and exile. As you will shortly discover this is an indisputable fact.

Some months before the incidents that I am recording here, there had been a major, cataclysmic disaster in our village. It really is not necessary or helpful for me to explain the nature of this disaster. I hardly understand it myself. In some ways the memory is even more dark and dreadful than that of my banishment, and I really do not wish to relive it. Suffice to say that our little community was violently torn apart to the point of fragmentation, and thrust into a claustrophobic depth of darkness that we could never have imagined. Then, quite unexpectedly, an opportunity for healing arose. We were, if I may put it like this, presented with a miraculous opportunity to move from chaos and darkness into a place of light and reconstruction. Such joy! And for a time I seemed to be as much a part of this process as were all the others. The drive towards regeneration involved the necessary forming and re-forming of groups as we discovered common ground and searched for connections that might eventually make us whole once more. It was not easy, but it was exciting, and I was excited.

Then, in a heart-stopping instant, it happened. With no warning whatsoever I was literally picked up, flown away from my village and deposited unceremoniously onto the very centre of the mysterious and terrible Vast

White Plain. I have already described the horror of my experiences there.

My return from the Vast White Plain was quite as impossible to predict as my exile had been. Inexplicably the entire universe seemed to be filled with what I can only describe as a mighty gasp. And then, amazingly, I was flying. In less than a second the motion had stopped and I found myself suspended, motionless, immediately above the place that I had always known as *my* world.

There below me, perfectly restored and ineffably harmonious, was my own dear village, bathed in summer sunshine. Even from that height I could clearly see the children playing on the green, and over there next to the Post Office the plump postman, chamois leather in hand, keen as ever to make his jolly red van gleam and sparkle. The dear, proud little robin sang from his perch on the railing. The old Horse and Groom seemed to beam benevolently across the glittering surface of the pond, its ancient brickwork warm and mellow in the golden rays of the sun. In that glorious moment I knew one thing for sure. An eternity of exile could never have shaken the belief in my heart that this was the place where I not only belonged but was truly needed.

It was perfect. Or rather, it was so *very nearly* perfect. I knew, without a trace of vanity, that my presence would make it perfect.

I wonder if you will understand me when I say that, as I began to make my final descent, I seemed to see the outline of my own destiny looming before me, and I experienced an unmistakable sense of being *held* and directed by a force much more powerful than myself. Eventually, as I slipped quietly and comfortably back into the part of our village that always had been rightfully and specifically mine, I swear to you that I heard a voice, proceeding, as it were, from somewhere in the heavens above me, and these are the words that were spoken.

'Look at this. I threw this bit in the box lid a couple of days ago because I couldn't see how that bright blue colour could possibly fit anywhere. I thought it must have got in there from some other puzzle. Turns out it's the groom's neckerchief thingy on the pub sign. I nearly chucked it in the bin. There we are. Finished.'

Endnotes

1. Plass, A., *Jesus – Safe Tender Extreme* (London: Zondervan, 2006).
2. Plass, A. and B., *The Son of God is Dancing* (Milton Keynes: Authentic Media Limited, 2005).
3. Plass, A., *Father to the Man and Other Stories* (London: Marshall Pickering, 1998).
4. Tournier, P., *A Place for You* (SCM-Canterbury Press, 1970).

Seriously Funny

Life, Love and God . . .
Musings Between Two
Good Friends

Adrian Plass and
Jeff Lucas

Having delighted, amused and challenged thousands of readers around the world for many years with their individual titles, Adrian Plass and Jeff Lucas are now ready to let their readers in on their private correspondence. As Adrian says in his first letter, 'If we were pushed into a corner and forced to be absolutely straight about our religion, what kind of truth would emerge?'

This book is the answer to that question. It is a joy to read, funny, sad, controversial and, above all, honest.

978-1-85078-869-0

**Bacon Sandwiches
and Salvation**

*An A-Z of the
Christian Life*

Adrian Plass

What are the two most important things in the universe? Bacon sandwiches and salvation, suggests Adrian Plass.

In this book, you'll find out why. Humorous definitions, outrageously rewritten hymns and choruses, along with more thoughtful or poignant pieces, provide a collection that will make you laugh, cry – and reflect. Vintage Plass.

'Doubt: more or less frequent visitor who should be allowed in when he knocks at the door and sat firmly down in a corner. As long as he is neither fed nor entertained he will usually get bored after a while and go away.'

'Go in peace: (1) injunction to the congregation at the end of communion (2) something that is only possible for those blessed with an en-suite bathroom and toilet.'

'Pillar of the church: big thick thing that holds everything up and restricts vision.'

978-1-85078-723-5

Silences and Nonsenses

Collected Poetry, Doggerel and Whimsy

Adrian Plass

Adrian Plass has been delighting readers with his poetry for more than twenty-five years, and this book finally brings it all together in one volume. As he says, 'To have them all, good, not so good, simple, complicated, light-hearted, funny, serious, sensible and silly collected into one volume is more exciting that I can say.'

Funny, poignant, challenging and sometimes downright hysterical – these poems will delight readers. Some were born from times of incredible personal difficulty. Others have come from his visits to dangerous and poor parts of the world. Others come from his love affair with the Church. All of them reflect the man, his faith, his life and his joy.

978-1-85078-876-8

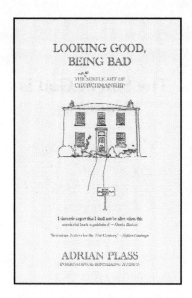

Looking Good, Being Bad

The Not So Subtle Art of Churchmanship

Adrian Plass

Have you ever wondered how and why the body of Christ is constantly tripping over itself to derail its mission and ward off the world? Or have you ever marvelled at how those less spiritual than yourself can be in positions of leadership? Have you ever had that niggling sense that some other force was at work in that committee meeting? You are not alone. All is revealed in this annual report from Churchmanship Headquarters in Great Malvern, the training ground for all who would carry on the noble tradition of thwarting the work of the gospel among us.

Looking Good, Being Bad gently challenges the churchman or woman in us all as we go about making the church in our own image. Plass's humour heals even as it cuts to the heart of our motivations with its knife-edge of truth.

978-1-85078-898-0